A Wood-Fired

CHRISTMAS

A Wood-Fired
CHRISTMAS

MADDIE EVANS

Philangelus Press
Boston, MA

ISBN: 978-1-942133-54-4

Cover art by Skye Winter

Editing by Jane Lebak

CHAPTER ONE

Ezra Blake belted out lyrics that might have been considered "in tune with the radio" as long as there weren't any listeners. In an empty pizzeria, there weren't. With speakers blaring, singing words he knew by heart, he shot his pizza peel into the brick oven and snaked out a hot cheese pizza with mushrooms and meatballs. He barely noticed the aroma of seasoned ground beef and the hiss of cooked semolina as it slid into the box. Ezra sliced it, set the plastic table on the center, and sealed it up. He tucked the box over the oven to stay warm, then retrieved the second pizza.

The jangle of the shop door silenced his singing but left the music untouched. Ezra didn't look toward whoever had come in. Even if he had a customer, pizzas in an 800-degree wood-fired oven cooked in ninety seconds.

Customers could wait. Burning a pizza would be a crime.

Finally, with the second pie tucked atop the oven, Ezra turned and found himself facing the gray-haired, poloshirt-wearing shop owner. "Barrett," Ezra said automatically, not immediately registering the red-headed woman at the owner's side.

The red-headed *young* woman.

Seriously, she could have been Barrett's granddaughter. And she was gorgeous. Sure, he was rich, but did he have to bring his arm candy into the shop?

As Ezra fumbled to turn off the music, Barrett waved him down with a laugh. "Go on doing what you're doing, just like the master you are." He turned to the young woman. "As you've probably guessed, this is Ezra, who does everything."

Yeah, *everything* except dating a woman who could be his granddaughter—which, to be fair, would be impossible on the grounds that Ezra was only twenty-five.

Instead of talking to Barrett and his cute date (the mischievous sort of cute), Ezra wiped down the pizza peel with a dry cloth, then raked inside the wood-fired oven to make sure everything stayed at a good burn. This oven was a marvel, able to retain heat forever, but even so, he chucked in another log and tucked it toward the back.

By the time he'd finished, an actual customer had arrived. Barrett made himself useful by running the customer's card and handing over those previous two pizzas, probably trying to impress on the young woman that although he was an absentee owner, Barrett Lovelace wasn't exactly useless. He just chose to be useful somewhere else most of the time.

When the door closed behind the customer, Ezra returned to the counter. "You guys want anything?"

Barrett beamed. "Relax! I just wanted to introduce you to Lacey." When Ezra glanced at her, Barrett added, "She'll be the new owner."

———— ✦ ————

The new owner.

The new owner...of Loveless Pizza?

Ezra shook Lacey's hand while the pieces fitted together in his mind the same way a pizza gets assembled on the line. Dough, followed by sauce, followed by cheese, followed by toppings, followed by ninety seconds in the oven, followed by boxing up. Words, followed by meaning, followed by implications, followed by...

"You're selling the place?" Ezra's mouth was dryer than the sun-dried tomatoes.

Barrett laughed. "I'm getting too old for this. It's time, you know?"

No, he didn't know. How could it be time for Barrett to get rid of the place when he'd never done anything with it from the start...? When Ezra had been the only reason the pizzeria survived at all...? When from the beginning, it had been nothing but a hole in the wall...until Ezra turned it into a hole in the wall to be proud of?

Lacey still hadn't said anything, which was fine because Ezra didn't want to hear her. He wanted to pepper Barrett with a hundred questions, except the only one that came out was, "What makes it time?"

Barrett shrugged. "I'm an old man, and we both know I'm not doing everything with this place that it could be. Lacey bounced some ideas off me, and I decided it's her turn."

Ezra glanced at her again. Short. Red-headed. Clever-eyed. Smiling.

Well, why shouldn't she be smiling? She was about to own Loveless Pizza.

9

Was Ezra being fired? Was he about to look for a job with a month to go before Christmas?

Barrett looked unconcerned, which of course he would be because he had all the money in the world. "I'll get the paperwork done over the next month, but she'll take over in my place for now, and I figure by New Year's, we'll have Lacey all set up and ready to go."

Five weeks.

Why her? Why had Barrett never said anything about getting out of the business? Except what good would it have done if he had, given that Ezra could never have afforded to buy the place? This job had been the difference between living in his car and living in a rented bedroom, but that tip jar wouldn't fund taking over the establishment.

Ezra should do something, say something, muster a smile. "Congratulations," he forced out, only then the phone rang, thank goodness, and he grabbed it so he could take the order. Sixty seconds later, he was staring at a receipt full of writing he couldn't remember scrawling on it, but indicating three pizzas that needed assembling.

One, two, three. November, December, January.

He looked up to find Lacey sitting on one of exactly two stools. She had her elbows on the counter, as she watched Ezra smear on the tomato sauce.

He said, "Deciding if you'll fire me?"

She offered a smile. "I figured the only things that got fired here were the pizzas."

Hah. Ezra said, "Why would you want to buy a pizzeria?" More to the point, why *this* pizzeria? "Do you work in the restaurant industry?"

She nodded. "A bit."

Awesome. Loveless Pizza was about to go straight down a ditch.

Well, maybe not. Barrett hadn't known a single thing about pizza the day he'd opened Loveless, and as far as Ezra knew, he hadn't learned anything since. Lacey might do exactly the same thing, and after she'd finished patting herself on the back for owning a pizzeria—as if she'd just earned her twentieth merit badge—she'd stop by once a month to impress her friends and make sure the business hadn't closed.

Barrett returned with one of their paper menus and was talking up a storm to Lacey about the different options and things she could change. Enlightened self interest was the only thing that prevented Ezra from asking if they'd both lost their minds. You don't come into a successful business and change things on day one before you know anything about it.

Ezra had been here on the literal day one, leaning into the front door with a key that thunked open a reluctant lock, then flipping on the lights to discover every bulb but one was burnt out. He'd explored the whole place and figured it was a sinking ship, but at the same time, he'd needed it to sail, so he'd climbed aboard.

The changes *he'd* made were all good changes, though. Changes like "changing the light bulbs" and "changing the name on the electric bill to Barrett Lovelace." And then, slowly, changing their reputation in Hartwell, Maine until people actually liked ordering from them.

Ezra said, almost to himself, "We were voted the number one pizza in the region last year."

Lacey nodded. "I saw that."

Barrett and Lacey sat at one of the two tables, their

11

laptops open and Lacey taking notes the whole time. Ezra kept working on orders, and their driver—his sister Shelly —spent two minutes in the shop to pick up the next delivery.

Ezra returned to the oven and the flaming wood. Everything was about to change before Christmas, but the only real change was Lacey.

CHAPTER TWO

Lacey couldn't read Ezra's face, but Uncle Barrett thought he was wonderful. Uncle Barrett also had... Well, opticians around the world would love to patent his rose-colored glasses, so you never really knew what Uncle Barrett was seeing versus what was there.

Still, when Lacey had learned about the operation of Lovelace Pizza, Uncle Barrett had kept answering her questions with, "You'll have to ask Ezra."

Ezra had looked like joy itself when she'd first seen him through the shop window, music vibrating the chilly glass while he moved with a fluidity she'd never expected from someone manipulating doughy circles on what was, in effect, a big wooden oar. That whole kitchen, and only one man—but he dominated it. He dominated it with his music and his voice and his movement, the way he managed the phone and the oven and the pizzas all at the same time.

At least, he'd looked like joy until the moment Uncle Barrett said she'd be taking over. Then he'd looked like revulsion.

Lovelace Pizza seemed indistinguishable from every other hole in the wall pizzeria Lacey had graced during high school, college, and the three years afterward. When her marketing job had announced layoffs, Uncle Barrett had offered this place to her, but what had she gotten herself into? It had two tables, two stools by the counter, a website that made her phone shed sparkling electronic tears, and an order system older than her freshman dorm at the University of Maine in Bangor.

What Uncle Barrett did have, however, were meticulous records. When Lacey had a financial question, he produced the answer within seconds, so she'd known from the start exactly how many employees they had (as opposed to how many they could afford) and what they spent on product versus what they took daily in sales, how many pizzas they made per day (that was capped, for some reason,) and so on.

It was the other stuff Uncle Barrett couldn't answer, like when she said, "Why don't you use more fresh organic produce?" and "Why don't you sell things other than pizzas?" and "Where are you advertising?" Even after her freshman year of college, she'd known the importance of advertising, and yet, somehow, Uncle Barrett didn't.

Still, Lacey could make this work. Within a year, she'd have it operating in the black, and it would be the first place anyone in Hartwell thought about when they thought of pizza. Next time, it wouldn't be a local newspaper that voted them best in the region. They'd be getting write-ups in magazines or even camera crews from TV shows.

Uncle Barrett took a phone call, so Lacey returned to the counter. Ezra was cleaning equipment by the sink. She said, "You run the place solo?"

Ezra had a voice dusky as a sunset. "Usually. There's a part-timer, but when he's here, he runs it solo, too."

Lacey said, "George?"

Ezra's voice flattened. "Greg."

She nodded. "Why only a hundred pizzas a day?"

Ezra looked annoyed. "That was Barrett's decision before we even opened. A hundred doughs a day, and then we close."

Lacey said, "Don't people get upset when they call and they can't get a pizza?"

Ezra looked over his shoulder. "That's what I said, but Barrett wanted everything laid back. If they want something from us, they call it in early."

Lacey's nose wrinkled. Ezra added, "Since he wouldn't budge on the hundred doughs a day, I made it a selling point."

This was what Lacey meant about the rose colored glasses. If the place was hopping, why not sell two hundred pizzas? Although Ezra kept calling them "doughs," so maybe she should, too. Instead of pressing on that, she said, "Why do you keep calling it *Loveless*?"

Ezra laughed for the first time. "You want the classy answer, or the real answer?"

Lacey tilted her head. "The real answer isn't classy?"

"When you're talking to a newspaper, the answer is, it's 'Loveless' because that's how the poet Robert Lovelace is pronounced."

Lacey said, "Except it's Barrett Love-Lace, so..."

Ezra gave a quick roll of his eyes. "The real answer is, when you're in the middle of the dinner crush and getting a phone call every two minutes and a pizza coming out of the oven every thirty seconds, people hear you answer the phone with 'loveless' and it turns out, *Maine-ahs* think that's funny."

Lacey's mouth twitched. "You could correct them."

"I'm not fighting a customer about something that unimportant, and I'm a Mainer, too, so I also think it's funny. Last Valentine's Day, I did a one-day special on an actual 'loveless' pizza. Personal pan sized."

Lacey snorted. "What on earth did you use for the toppings?"

"Sadness and spite," Ezra said because just then the phone rang, and he took another order.

Uncle Barrett, of course, had called it 'Love-lace' Pizza every time he called it anything at all. Usually, though, it was "my pizzeria" because he was tickled that he actually owned one.

Sadness and spite, though... Anchovies and pineapple would give a lovely sense of salty tears and acidic loneliness while being nauseating enough that no one would order the thing. Fun as a menu option, less fun from a profit and loss perspective.

Ezra told the caller, "Ready in twenty minutes," and returned to assembling pizzas. He was fast, rolling them round, tossing the dough overhead a few times, then covering it with a ladle full of sauce. On went the cheese. On went the toppings, one after the next. Into the oven went the first, then the second, then the third. Every motion was smooth, almost prescient. His hands moved without him checking what he was grabbing.

For a "Loveless" pizza, Ezra still seemed to love what he was doing. Lacey already liked the shop, and she'd only been here fifteen minutes. He'd worked here for years, so love would make some degree of sense. Wouldn't you have to love it to trudge to work every day in a building like this?

But how much more could this operation become? Why weren't they selling wings? Why only two little tables? Why not have outdoor seating and more menu options?

As Ezra slid a pizza into the wood-fired oven, Lacey mused, "We could add more toppings to the menu."

Ezra's face tightened, but he said nothing.

Uncle Barrett returned. "Oh, good, you and Ezra are getting to know one another. Ezra's our backbone, and you're going to take over as the head, so I think we're good."

Ezra glanced up. "And the arms and legs?"

Uncle Barrett chuckled. "That takes care of itself. What matters is, the bones are good, and you two are going to make this a success."

CHAPTER THREE

"It's already a success!" Ezra ranted at the speakerphone while driving home. "The food is good. The bills get paid. The customers are loyal. And she pirouettes in dictating changes...? What does she even know?"

His sister said, "Before you go to war, take a deep breath. Okay, so she's being a brat. Give Miss Rich Buyer Girl a week, and I bet she'll do just what Barrett does and cash her checks without opening the door."

"I didn't get that impression. She thinks she's going to stomp in and save the place—which, you'll notice, doesn't need saving."

"What other reason is there to buy a restaurant, except to save it?" The way Shelly snorted, he could hear her roll her eyes even over the phone. "But seriously, is it possible the place isn't doing as well as you think?"

"I do *everything* there."

"Everything except filing the taxes and writing payroll and monitoring the bank balance. You know the *stuff* that's coming in and going out, but you're not writing the checks." Shelly hesitated. "You know, the way Mom always seemed to have money coming in, and yet...?"

Ezra huffed. "Fine."

"You need to figure out if both of us need a different job."

Shelly didn't really "work" for Loveless Pizza. She popped in to deliver pizzas when she wasn't taking classes. She could deliver pizzas for anyone.

Ezra could make pizzas for anyone, too. But he knew Loveless. He'd set up everything to work the way he wanted it to. Barrett pretended to be in charge, but in point of fact, Barrett always let Ezra do whatever he wanted because Ezra had made the place successful.

The whole "one hundred doughs a day" cap had seemed like lunacy, so Ezra did the thing you always did with something dumb and phrased it like an incredible opportunity. Ezra had set up their social media with an automated countdown, and when they got to twenty-five pizzas remaining, the different accounts posted one of several rotating messages. (Shelly had a way with snark, so some of the messages were funny. "I hope you're committed to intermittent fasting. Only five pies left.")

"Fear of missing out," people called it, and Ezra worked that angle hard. "Order your Loveless Pizza early so there's no love lost!"

Lacey was going to change it back to "Love-lace" and destroy the whole gimmick because she didn't understand.

Shelly said, "Look, there's one thing you do really well, and that's—"

Ezra pulled into his driveway. "Making pizza."

"—it's operating under pressure, you dork. You never lose your cool, not even when you get like thirty-five orders at the same time." Shelly laughed. "Pretend this woman is a fifty-pizza order that's got to be on the table in twenty minutes. Keep calm. Get analytical. Make a plan of attack."

Ezra shut off the engine and frowned as he stared at the carved-up Victorian where he rented a room. "Maybe more like a nor'easter."

"Better analogy. You've got a month to plan for the storm. What do you need to weather it? What are the things that might get blown around? What's most important and needs to be secured? What's most at risk of getting buried?"

Ezra pulled his phone from the holder but didn't leave the car. "So, Hurricane Lacey is en route. We need bottled water and canned goods, and we need full batteries in all the electronics."

"You need gas in the car. And you need a go-bag."

The go-bag equivalent was getting another job. "I don't want to leave."

That was the crux. Barrett wanted to leave, but Ezra didn't.

Lacey wanted to stay. Still, give it a month. The weeks between Thanksgiving and Christmas were a wringer. Maybe after that, she wouldn't want to buy the place after all.

Even so. Ezra said, "If Barrett was going to sell the place to someone, it should have been me."

Shelly said, "I'll help you look for change in the couch."

Ezra didn't even own a couch. With a sigh, he got out of the car.

Lacey arrived at Lovelace Pizza to find Ezra in shirtsleeves and already at work making dough. Again, he moved with a control and smoothness that left her shivering.

Get a grip. He was about to be her employee. The last thing she needed was for him to feel like she was checking him out, so she'd better quit checking him out.

He looked up with a frown creasing his forehead. So serious. For a moment, she shivered again, this time at the intensity in his expression. Could this man see her soul? Was he actually human, or was he instead a forest elemental her uncle had summoned by accident while sipping whiskey and playing cards with his friends?

That did sound like the kind of thing Uncle Barrett would stumble into. Instead of winning a pizzeria in a poker game, he'd won ownership over one of the fae, and when it turned out Uncle Barrett had no idea what to do with an otherworldly servant, the Fairy King had replied, "Well, I make decent pizza."

Ezra certainly had the eyes for it. What was it people said about the fae, that they could use "glamour" on unsuspecting humans? Ezra probably had that.

Lacey removed her backpack. "What do you need me to do?"

Ezra stared her down. "I wasn't aware I needed you to do anything."

"I need to learn everything you do, but it doesn't make sense for me just to watch if I can help."

Ezra's eyes got wide as she pulled a canvas apron from her backpack. "You're serious?"

She glanced at her apron. Was he surprised it was black? His was white, or at least it had started out white. Now it was whatever color you'd call semolina and flour and tomato sauce and a thousand other splotches after hot water ceased evicting them all. She said, "It's neat thinking of all the pizzas your apron has seen."

That was the first moment Lacey saw anything on Ezra's face other than control. It was a wild mix of overwhelm and disbelief. He hadn't counted on meeting her this morning. Or maybe ever, given how Uncle Barrett described the business. Maybe like a true fairy king, he'd been planning on whistling a tune like a cartoon magician and having the pizza doughs knead themselves, only she'd interrupted.

Ezra said, "Everything's under control, so you might as well watch."

She sat on a stool with a notebook, and Ezra returned to his work.

The man operated like a machine, not a preternatural visitor to the human realm. While prepping, he shut her out completely and got his stations set up. Set up for one person, she realized. Uncle Barrett claimed to come in "pretty often," but Ezra seemed to have had no such illusion that a second person would come. Instead, he'd set up a twelve-by-twelve work area to accommodate everything within arm's reach. One tiny kitchen, one walk-in, one minuscule office, and one monster of a wood-fired oven. Behind him, a mixer churned dough while Ezra heated pots of sauce and set up stations for toppings. Lacey noted everything he did, including the time when a truck pulled up to the back door and unloaded supplies. Lacey recorded the delivery guy's name. (Ezra greeted him with, "Hey, Max," and Max just grunted.) The large mixer had a name, too: "the Hobart." Ezra ignored Lacey while turning the Hobart's massive mound of dough into pizza-sized balls that would stand to rise.

Lacey set aside her notebook to stack the delivery items. The walk-in had a precision to its setup, and she made sure to add new product to the back and push the older product forward so it would get used first. She did the same on the storage shelves. Ezra let her do this in silence, only glancing at her every so often.

It would be nice if he talked. He had a dusky voice, but she'd only ever heard a few sentences.

At some point, he checked everything over, then frowned as if puzzled. He said, "You've messed up my system. It went faster because you handled restocking."

As Lacey set that in her notebook, she said, "Is that a problem?"

"I'm not used to downtime." He huffed. "Are you going to dock my pay for half an hour of daydreaming?"

"Don't even joke. My former manager used to say if I had time to lean, I had time to clean." As Ezra approached, looking at her notebook, she showed him what she'd been writing. "You're super efficient. I don't see anything I can improve."

He huffed. "Did I ask you to improve anything?"

Those eyes of his were piercing. Lacey said, "Sometimes a newcomer can see flaws in the system."

Ezra drew breath, but then he said nothing. Instead he found one of the ubiquitous kitchen-things that needed to be done and turned his back on her.

Lacey called, "If you need unskilled labor, I can assemble pizza boxes."

"You're going to be the boss. I usually assemble them as needed because there's not much room."

In terms of understatements, that was magnificent. Lacey said, "I wonder if we could make more room in here by repositioning the equipment."

"If you're thinking of hanging the Hobart off the ceiling,

no." Ezra sounded unamused.

"No, but with more space, we could be selling wings or cheesy bread." She glanced around. "And more toppings."

Ezra said, "Why?"

She stepped into the center of the kitchen and swiveled. "The wood-fired oven is great, but we're under-utilizing the stovetop. We could be offering more and better options."

He set his jaw. "Our customers don't think the options are sub-par."

"Except for the ones who want a greater variety and therefore don't become our customers." She turned back to Ezra. His dark eyes were lit up with that earlier intensity. "We could open a whole new world to them. I'd love to offer farm-to-table pizzas."

His voice was thin. "Are you out of your mind? Did you forget we're in Maine?"

She huffed. "There's sustainable eating in Maine."

Ezra said, "Sustainable eating is an unsustainable business practice. Have you looked into what that would require?"

Again, his voice was beautiful, but the anger undercutting it was making him less attractive.

She nodded. "One of my previous jobs made an arrangement with the local farms so we could offer seasonal produce."

"And how much do we get?" Ezra stepped toward her. "How many of these can we sell? What do we do with the extras? How long can they stay fresh?" He gestured at the rest of the kitchen. "I can tell you how much of any topping we need for every day of the week, but if Farmer Bill shows up with a trunk full of onions, what am I supposed to do with that?"

Lacey tilted her head. "So we offer a daily special."

"The pizza grab-bag? Blind date with a pizza?" He pivoted away, then turned back. His eyes were even more livid. "You'll pop in with a bag of zucchini, and it'll be my job to figure out how to sell twenty zucchini-topped pizzas?"

She raised her hands. "Only toppings you'd expect on a pizza—but locally-sourced."

Ezra pointed to the walk in. "That's local enough for me."

Lacey sighed. "There's something special about food that remembers the field it came from."

He rolled his eyes so hard it was a shock he didn't sprain them. "Most people would prefer their food not remember anything at all. Do we also do farm-to-table ground beef for the meatballs? Today's Loveless farm-to-table special used to be named Bessie. We even made the mozzarella with her milk."

Lacey recoiled. "Wow. That's awful."

He lowered his voice. "Is there something I should know about the finances? Because if bankruptcy is around the corner, I need to find another job now."

Lacey paused. "How'd we get from torturing innocent cattle to bankruptcy?"

Ezra folded his arms. "You're storming in here talking about making it more efficient and changing things up when it's working fine. Did Barrett sell it to you because he wanted to jump off a sinking ship?"

For the first time, Lacey realized what she was seeing in Ezra's eyes. It wasn't just intensity. It was resentment. She blurted out, "Why are you angry at me?"

"You're changing things you don't understand. Pizza isn't about the gourmet experience—or maybe some places it is, but not *our* pizza." He took a ragged breath, as though steadying himself. "People want to know what they're getting, and they want it in a reasonable time frame. It's cheap, and it's fast, and it's the same every time. We are not changing anyone's life. But we might be changing someone's evening by making it easier."

Lacey spread her hands. "But we can make it memorable, too. We can make it better for the environment."

Ezra said, "By destroying our customer base? We've already got a niche."

She waved a hand. "We don't need to stay in a hole like a mole rat. We can branch out. Maybe expand our offerings, maybe offer more than a hundred pizzas a day."

Ezra said, "You're going to destroy the place."

Lacey's breath caught, and she stared into Ezra's eyes.

He was intense, sure, but this time, she didn't look away.

A thousand responses blazed in her mind, but the one she snapped out was, "Or maybe I'll realize its potential the way you never did."

CHAPTER FOUR

Kitchen work didn't pay well, so Ezra knew he had a good deal with Loveless.

When Barrett had won the pizzeria in a game of cards, he'd taken it on more as a lark than anything else. Having worked in finance, he hadn't known abusing the cooks was the industry standard.

Instead, with an unseriousness Ezra would later come to recognize as Barrett's signature attitude, he'd decided it would be fun to close out his career owning a pizzeria. How hard could it be?

"Help Wanted. Full time. Let's make pizzas! Two guys, one kitchen, one hundred pizzas a day. Simple toppings. We close when we sell out, but you get paid for the full day. We'll split tips."

Ezra, in desperate need, decided this place would go down the tubes in three months, but three months of income was three months more than zero, so he applied. Once they opened, he actually enjoyed it. Barrett had started out doing as much work as Ezra, but then it was less, and less, and less, and that hands-off approach laid a lot of work on Ezra's shoulders. By the end, Ezra had needed to manage it all, so he'd figured it out.

It was the same way he'd figured everything out all his life. With your back to the wall, the only way to go was forward, so forward he went.

He got paid the full day no matter how long he worked, so it made sense to sell out sooner. That was his first impulse, but then he realized selling out was selling out—and that meant income for the business. He prepped in the mornings while listening to audiobooks about advertising and Ted Talks about the psychology of marketing. He finessed the social media to make it fun. He offered deals to large-scale customers and made connections. Ezra really leaned into the idea of "The Loveless One Hundred."

Loveless even did a few charity events for free (Barrett had been no-holds-barred gung-ho for those). Eventually, Hartwell figured out who they were.

Not bad for three years of backbreaking, soul-sweating effort.

Effort which Lacey intended to gut in a matter of weeks.

Another job wouldn't be hard to find. What would be hard to find was another job with this flexibility and these hours and the people he'd come to know. Another job where Ezra's personality and the business's reputation were so closely linked.

Ezra hadn't grown up in Hartwell. No one knew him as a trailer park kid with five younger siblings, all wearing shoes they'd outgrown nine months before. He'd created an online persona for the business, but he'd grown into it, or maybe the business had grown into him. Customers chatted with Ezra as though they knew him. They'd make jokes over the phone that they'd seen first on their social media. They'd start their calls with, "Am I in time?" and sometimes Ezra even answered the phone with, "Hey, you're one of the Loveless One Hundred!"

The hour before Barrett had escorted Lacey into the shop, Ezra had been contemplating t-shirts saying exactly that. "We are the Loveless One Hundred."

The Love-lace One Hundred-and-Sixty-One wouldn't have the same ring.

He was going to watch his business go down the tubes.

He was going to need another job.

"You have us open on Thanksgiving."

Lacey sounded irritated, as though Ezra couldn't read a calendar. With a glance up, he said, "We are."

Her nose wrinkled (and it made her look cute) while she stared at the laptop screen. "Why?"

Ezra swept out a hand toward the dozens of dough balls proofing on the counter. "See, we sell pizzas, and we can't do that if we're closed."

She shook her head and waved him down. "Yes, yes, I get that part. But who buys pizza for Thanksgiving?" She half rolled her eyes. "Or do you sell a turkey and cranberry sauce pizza?"

Ezra tried to give her a patient look, but mostly to hide the inner flinch because...well...yes. Kind of. "It turns out a lot of people don't celebrate Thanksgiving on the actual day, but they also don't feel like cooking." He spoke louder so she couldn't interrupt him. "We keep it to sixty doughs that day, but we do sell out. You can check the records."

This was her second day in the shop. Thanksgiving was

this week, so while she'd probably been planning on a short week, Ezra didn't have Thanksgiving off. He didn't need it, didn't want it, and never had taken it.

"Wait, the grocery store?" Lacey chuckled. "We delivered three pies to the grocery store? Oh, and the rehab hospital. I wouldn't have thought that. Wouldn't their kitchen have made a real Thanksgiving dinner for the residents?"

"Early delivery for the morning shift before they go."

"Makes sense." Then she stiffened, and Ezra braced himself. "Wait, you actually put together a Thanksgiving pizza?"

"Turkey sausage, onions, and mushrooms." He checked the sauce as it heated. "I didn't go too crazy with it, like using gravy or dotting it with mashed potatoes and cranberry sauce."

"I'm...speechless." She did seem momentarily speechless, but before Ezra could enjoy the effect, she said, "And this year?"

He nodded. "You can see people have already ordered a bunch, plus a few orders will come in organically. You know, people who do the turkey on Friday or Saturday and want a break, or folks who celebrate alone."

Lacey said, "That's an idea. Maybe next year, we can throw a pizza party for people who have nowhere to go."

How would he even advertise that? "Isolated? Bored out of your mind? Have a Loveless Thanksgiving!" Although if Lacey's vision came true, it wouldn't be Ezra's problem next year...assuming it was anyone's problem.

He said, "It'll be a quiet day. I can handle it solo."

She frowned, and again, it was almost cute. "That's not fair. Then you don't get a Thanksgiving."

Ezra shrugged. "I don't mind."

It wasn't that he didn't mind. Ezra had nowhere to go. The first year, Barrett hadn't noticed that Ezra opened on Thanksgiving because Barrett had flown off to feast with his second cousins who owned a mansion in California wine country—and, not coincidentally, a nationally-known winery. Ezra had called some places he knew would be open (eg, the Hartwell Fire Department, who laughed at him because they'd already planned a nine-course turkey dinner) and mustered up a few pity orders from managers who wanted to boost the morale of whatever skeleton crew they could muster. Finally he'd posted to social media, expecting derision like Lacey's, except a few people replied with, "Top that thing with turkey, and I'm ordering."

He and Shelly had done all the deliveries, then once he'd closed for the day, he and she had eaten the sixty-first pizza at the counter. "It's better than Mom would have done," Shelly had remarked, and Ezra had snorted because he could have opened a can of turkey-flavored cat food and surpassed anything Mom would have done.

The next year, he'd used turkey sausage, and the pizza was even better—plus, they'd gotten a reputation.

Lacey said, "You'll celebrate your Thanksgiving on Saturday or Sunday, then? When Greg's working?"

Ezra snapped, "I said I'll be fine." Then, to soften things, "What are you doing for Thanksgiving?"

She tilted her head. "You don't do Thanksgiving at all? What about Shelly?"

About to reply, he stopped. Then, "My family doesn't do Thanksgiving."

She said, "Moral objection?"

"Financial objection. Space objection. Can we change the subject?"

Lacey didn't reply, but her deep frown meant she wasn't letting it go. He said again, "What are you doing?"

She huffed. "Well, normally I'd be in Boston with my family, but this year, Uncle Barrett wants me to join him."

Ezra blurted out, "What?" She looked up, and he said, "Barrett's your uncle?"

His whole body had gone numb. He stood leaning on a counter he couldn't feel beneath his hands. Uncle? Barrett was conceding the place to Lacey not because she had any business running a pizzeria, but because she was his *niece*?

This wasn't even like Barrett trying to impress a hot date or picking up a gold digger. Nepotism was the worst reason to do anything. No one was ever qualified when that happened.

Sounding confused, Lacey said, "Yeah—? Didn't I say that?"

"No! He just said you were 'Lacey' and you never called him anything at all." Come to think of it, she'd been a master of never directly addressing Barrett in any fashion. It had always been "we" when she spoke about the place, or "he" when she meant Barrett.

Lacey said, "What's wrong?"

What was wrong? Other than they were doomed?

Ezra lowered his voice a notch. "I assumed you were buying the place because you had restaurant experience."

"I do have some," she said.

Forcing himself, he turned away and checked on the oven. The wood at the center had a good burn going, and he grabbed the tools to scatter the logs to the edges. "Your actual qualification is being his niece. If he'd been running a pottery shop, he'd have sold you that, and the same if he was printing a magazine about collector's edition soda cans."

Lacey made no reply.

He said, "Is he actually selling it to you? Or is he giving it to you?"

Lacey swallowed hard. "Giving it. He said he didn't pay for it, so neither should I."

Ezra shoved the logs backward, scattering sparks. The brick oven was heating well, a good toasty burn that made summers a nightmare but winters a comfort as it produced a pizza seared to perfection.

Lacey didn't love pizza. Barrett had loved pizza, or rather, he'd loved the charm. He'd gotten it running and left it alone, at least until the moment he'd balled it up and effectively tossed it in the the trash. Lacey didn't love it. She'd come onboard to change it.

So—organic onions for the Thanksgiving pizza? Or was she going to show up on Wednesday with a free range turkey that had died of old age?

From behind him, Lacey said, "Do you not have any family other than Shelly?"

"None that want to give me their pizzeria." Ezra went to get another log, but Lacey had moved to stand in front of the wood. "Do you mind?"

"I do mind. Do you have other family?"

"Not that it matters, but yes, I have two younger brothers and three younger sisters, and everyone else lives in a trailer out in Lewiston." He pointed to the wood, and Lacey stepped aside. "As you can imagine, we didn't have a rich uncle to give us a house. I saved up for a car because it made a handy spare bedroom, and even better, I drove it away."

Lacey said, "And you came here?"

"I bounced around." Ezra tucked two new logs into the oven and pushed them to the back. They'd start burning, and that should keep things right for a good long while. "When I found this place, I rented an actual room."

Lacey murmured, "Oh."

"So I guess your uncle bailed me out, too."

"He didn't bail me out. I did go to college." Lacey's voice was soft. "But I guess it looks that way."

Ezra held his hand in the mouth of the oven enough to gauge the temperature. The bricks had begun absorbing enough heat that they were reflecting it back into the interior. "If he'd offered, I might have been able to get a loan and pay it off over time, but with a family member around, I guess it's Merry Christmas for you."

Who was Ezra kidding? No payment plan on earth would have worked with his budget. *Time for September's payment, First Hartwell Mutual Cooperative Bank! I'll just check the tip jar to see if anyone left me a thousand dollar bill.*

Lacey's voice was soft. "He never mentioned any of this to you?"

"You were a Christmas surprise. You should have shown up with a little red ribbon around your hair." He turned back. "Not that any of this matters. If you run the place into the ground, you've got a safety net."

Lacey said, "And you don't."

It wasn't mean, the way she said it. Nor was it pitying. She wasn't the Lady on the Hill, observing her peasant serf as he fed the fire with wood carved from her estate. It was a mere acknowledgment: she had a safety net, and he didn't. She could afford to fail. If Ezra couldn't afford his rent, by contrast, he'd have to sell stuff and then return to living in his car.

When she spoke again, though, her voice was a bit sharper. "That's why you don't want me making any changes. Because you think I'm going to mess up your life."

He glared at her. "Since you put it that way: yes."

Lacey had an infuriating, unnatural calmness. "It's not all about you."

"Mess up the pizzeria, mess up its reputation—and yes, mess up my life." Ezra forced a smile he hoped looked venomous. "So—in that case, it is all about me."

CHAPTER FIVE

On Thanksgiving morning, Lacey arrived before Ezra, and she checked her notebook with all the opening details.

Ezra hated her, but that was fine as the feeling had become mutual. Sure, she was the rich brat who was tromping in and conducting a business coup designed to leave the pizzeria in rubble within two months. If every detail of the above was wrong, well—not Ezra's job to make sure he got it right, was it? He only cared about making the same pizza the same way forever and ever.

The guy couldn't be much older than her. How could he already have given up on life?

Lovelace Pizza had so much potential. Why not fulfill some of it? Why scrape by, bored for thirty years, and then retire, wondering why you never did any of those cool things you'd dreamed of as a kid?

He and she had plotted out the larger orders and their delivery times yesterday at close, so the day's only question mark was how many individual orders would come in. Ezra had estimated based on last year's sales, giving a reasonable cushion for growth.

As Lacey set about opening cans, she thought, *Thanksgiving pizzas*. See, Ezra had it in him to step off the beaten path when necessary, but he wanted those limits clearly staked out. She assumed they would do "loveless" Valentine's Day pizzas again, so that made it twice a year. Would they open Christmas day with a mistletoe-topped pizza?

Was mistletoe poisonous? Maybe it was one of those plants where you could eat the berries but not the leaves. Lacey had no intention of finding out, but perhaps on December 24th, she would take a delivery of mistletoe.

For that matter, perhaps Ezra would make her a mistletoe pizza as a peace offering, and after she ate it, he'd say, "Oh, I forgot, you'd better call poison control."

No. He wouldn't hurt her, no matter how angry he got. For all that he looked dangerous, and for all that they worked together alone in a tiny space filled with knives and fire, she'd never felt afraid...other than feeling afraid that he misunderstood every single thing about her.

She wasn't rich. She didn't think she was a brat. This wasn't a business coup. And she had no intention of destroying the pizzeria by March.

When Ezra unlocked the door, he was startled to see her there. "I thought you were feasting with Uncle Barrett."

"Happy Thanksgiving to you, too." She forced a smile. "I want to see these turkey pizzas."

He pulled off his jacket, saying, "They look about the same as non-turkey pizzas. You don't have to stay."

He couldn't very well eject the soon-to-be-owner, so Lacey said, "I know," and kept prepping.

He had plenty of days here without her. She'd shadowed him, and she'd shadowed Greg, struggling to learn everything. Last Friday night, she'd shadowed them both even though the kitchen was too small for three. But watching the pair of them in action had been a marvel, almost choreographed except every moment was new and never to be repeated. Ezra could toss the dough in the air and spin it so it stretched into a circle. Greg would work the phones. One would prep a pizza and get it in the oven, and ninety seconds later, the other would have it out of the oven and into a box. One would be reading back toppings from a phone call while the other was assembling those toppings. With both of them doing this dance, there'd even been music.

Uncle Barrett said he'd worked with Ezra at the beginning. "He's so fast," Lacey had gushed. "He knows where everything is. When Greg puts something down, Ezra picks it up as though it was always there. You must have had a blast working with him."

Uncle Barrett had replied, "I never worked that way with him. I was too slow."

Lacey might never pick up the required speed, either. On busy nights, it might be faster for Ezra if she stayed out of his way. Today, though? With the orders sparse and the pizzas planned out? She'd give it a try.

Ezra watched as she set up the Hobart, although she wasn't sure if his silence meant he was angry, if he was watching her fail, or if she was doing everything correctly.

He wouldn't just let her fail—of that, she was sure. The pizzeria meant everything to him—more than she'd anticipated—and he had no problems pitching a fight about anything he thought she did wrong. If she'd forgotten an ingredient, Ezra wouldn't risk complaints from ten customers and another twenty stalking away in silence.

While the Hobart growled into action, they went to work on the toppings.

She said, "Are these our knives, or your knives?"

Ezra shook his head. "Not mine."

No further conversation. Lacey prompted, "Some chefs are particular about using only their own knives."

Ezra replied, "One assumes they used their own money to buy those particular knives, and so far, I've failed to inherit my uncle's kingdom."

Ah, right, just in case she'd forgotten he hated her, it was important to remind her he still did.

She knew what he got paid (not necessarily the tips, but she could estimate those) and surely it was enough for a knife. Maybe not one of those high-end forged blades that you got if you'd won the Nobel Prize in food, but a reliable knife.

It was just—why did he always assume she'd ridden down from a mountain top astride a white horse, accompanied by twelve ladies in waiting? If she had money in her bank account, it had come from paychecks, the same as his had, and those paychecks had come from working a job. Yes, even though she had rich relatives! Fancy that.

Or, rather, don't fancy it. Instead, she cut up more onions to caramelize them for the Thanksgiving pizzas.

Uncle Barrett had called her in October after a chat with his financial advisor. He'd wanted to retire, but during that meeting, he'd realized it would mean more to his nieces and nephews if he gave them money now rather than in twenty years when he died.

All her cousins had grabbed the cash. Lacey had always

loved Uncle Barrett, and her job would be doing layoffs soon, so she'd said, "Couldn't I just work with you at the pizzeria?" He'd responded by offering her not a job, but the whole operation.

That didn't make her evil. Why would Ezra think it did?

Conversation remained in utilitarian mode. *Behind you. Coming through. This is hot. That's enough.* Although he wouldn't sing in her presence, Ezra tuned the radio to the local independent station, a combination of classic rock, local bands, and some weird concoctions an intern dug up from the basement of a shuttered secondhand record store. The Beatles' *"I Want to Hold Your Hand,"* only in German. *Komm, gib mir deine hand.*

Good thing Ezra would never take her hand. He'd probably have reversed the lyrics. "Hey, go take away your hand."

The first order was going to the rehab hospital before Lovelace was even supposed to be open. The aroma of onion and turkey sausage filling the shop, and Lacey closed her eyes as she inhaled.

She could spread toppings, sure, but Ezra could toss a pizza dough and have it spread like a wheel, then catch it without tearing the dough before he sent it soaring again. Up, catch, up, catch. It was fast and amazing. Then the pizza went back onto the counter, and she'd start the toppings while he spread the next pizza.

He was much faster than she was, so he was also sending the doughs into and out of the ovens. Ezra kept the pizzas moving with a finesse that amazed her over and over. There wasn't a timer. Or, rather, the timer existed entirely in his head so it felt right to him, or he'd shuffle the pizzas within the oven so the first went to the back and then came toward the front when the next went in. They slid in soft and emerged crisp, cheese bubbling.

Would she ever be able to do that? To know without looking that the crust had reached precisely the right shade of black-speckled gold, or hear without thinking about it that the peel had exactly the right grittiness to keep the pizzas sliding properly? The *shhh* of pizza going into the oven, and the pop of wood burning, or the slight crinkle of the paper in the box as the pizza slid onto it with the cheese melted and the sauce beneath at several hundred degrees— these weren't familiar yet, but to Ezra, they all functioned together like a train engine as it powered across the landscape.

By contrast, Lacey got tugged along like the caboose. When the first delivery order was done, Ezra shoved all the pies into the thermal delivery case and said, "Since you're here, you can deliver them."

It was a four minute drive to the rehab hospital, and they rushed her inside while nurses and the rest of the staff hovered like vultures. The nursing supervisor called "Code Zed" over the loudspeaker. Lacey left with a $20 tip in her pocket.

"Turns out, they love us," she said on returning to the shop, and she handed Ezra the twenty. He shoved it into the tip jar, then pointed to the next order. "Can you deliver that? Shelly's car died, and it'll take a bit for her to get here."

Was Shelly planning to bike the pies all over town? Kind of hard to deliver without a car.

Lacey headed to the grocery store with a mix of plain and Thanksgiving pizzas. At the back entrance, she got ushered directly into the break room while the manager issued a page over the loudspeaker. "We're only open for another hour," the manager said, "but it's been a madhouse."

The manager tipped Lacey out of her own wallet even as employees started descending on the pizzas. Lacey said, "Last-minute shoppers?"

The manager said, "And people picking up pre-cooked dinners. After all that, none of the staff wants to go home and cook."

Tossing pizzas, Ezra had his back to her when she returned. Lacey headed around to where he could see her. "Do you want me to go grab Shelly?"

He working the dough. "That might make sense, but since you're here, you can keep doing the deliveries."

Lacey shook her head."That leaves Shelly alone for Thanksgiving."

Ezra scowled as he set aside one dough and started the next. "I told you, we don't celebrate."

"Even so." Ezra appeared to be setting up multiple pizzas to get all four into the oven one after the next. "If I'm doing deliveries, I can do a pick-up."

He didn't answer, but then an order came in through the online system, so she washed her hands and got to work.

He ignored her far too much. This wasn't sustainable, but then again, what she said didn't require an answer as far as he was concerned because he'd already answered her. Maybe he was just so in his pizza-making zone that he couldn't spare time for things like, "It's fine." But, come on. They were working together. They should at least be polite.

Orders came in, and orders went out. Tips went into the tip jar. This wasn't a bad way to spend the holiday. Uncle Barrett had been surprised she wanted to, but then again, he'd also been surprised to learn that Ezra opened on

Thanksgiving Day.

In the meantime, Lacey learned which other local organizations opened on the holiday. Sure, the rehab hospital couldn't send all the residents home for the day, but a hunting and fishing store remained open for business the whole time. A drug store chain was open, which made some degree of sense until she realized the pharmacy of that drug store chain was closed.

It felt unfair. None of those employees needed to be there. Was corporate worried that someone would have a shampoo emergency? Would Thanksgiving be ruined if a customer couldn't pick up another spool of monofilament fishing line?

In a way, it made sense that Ezra wanted to work. If a Thanksgiving pizza could serve as a light for someone who felt unappreciated and apart from their family during the holiday, then in a way, Lovelace Pizza made the world less "loveless."

In short: Ezra could be thoughtful when he wanted to. He just didn't want to be thoughtful to Lacey.

She delivered a pizza and a bottle of soda to a single dad, his two school-age children leaping on the couch while chanting, "Tur-key-piz-za!" That guy tipped her huge, as though she'd done him a massive favor. Based on the cheering when he shut the door, maybe she had. She delivered to an elderly woman who seemed to be living alone and who asked if Lacey would like to join her, then wished her a happy Thanksgiving. To balance that out was a guy who grabbed his pizza boxes, grunted as he checked the receipt, and slammed the door.

Back at Lovelace, Shelly's car was stopped almost, but not quite, in the alley behind the shop. Lacey parked so

46

Shelly could pull out around her, then stepped inside to find Shelly filmy like a ghost at the counter, and Ezra loading pizzas into their largest thermal bag.

Shelly was in the middle of saying, "So when the check engine light is flashing, that's a *good* thing, right? It means the car is super-duper happy?"

"Yeah, you're not going anywhere. Just answer the phone and make sure the customers know it'll be forty minutes until they get anything." Ezra turned to Lacey. "A local family has an oven disaster and twenty-two guests. I'd have Shelly do it, but—"

"I can do it," Shelly said, wobbling to a stand.

Lacey said, "You look like death warmed over—"

Ezra said, "Death in the wood-fired oven for thirty seconds."

"—and I don't want a worker's comp claim. I'll take it."

Lacey tried to lift the bag, but it didn't budge. Ezra chuckled. "I'm taking this, don't worry."

Shelly said, "You're not supposed to overload the bag."

Lacey said, "And there's two bags. I'll go with you."

That's how she ended up in the back of Ezra's sedan, a thermal bag of pizzas buckled into the seat at her side and another on her lap. Ezra pulled out. It had just started raining.

He said, "Thanks for not making Shelly drive. When she arrived, her hands were shaking."

"What happened to her?"

"Something that for sure is going to run a few hundred bucks at the mechanic." Ezra looked grim. "The engine kept dying at highway speed, and she'd drift down to like fifteen miles an hour while frantically trying to get it to start again."

Lacey said, "And she still wanted to work?"

"She was closer to here than home. I think she's nuts, but the Thanksgiving tips are usually good, so she wanted at least part of it. Is it okay if she leaves her car in the back until I can get it fixed?"

Possible answers:

- *No, Shelly has to drive the unsafe car somewhere else.*
- *No, just push the thing into a spot where it will probably get ticketed and towed.*
- *No, because with the car that close to the back door, I will have to walk an extra twenty steps.*

Actual answer: "Of course! Shelly's going to need a ride home tonight, too."

"I'll figure her out." Ezra looked grim. "She got the oil changed last week, and right after, the electrical system went all bizarre. The mechanic claims he didn't touch a thing and her car's just twenty years old, but come on. You expect me to believe it was total coincidence?"

Lacey sighed. "That stinks."

"I want him to order a pizza so I can burn the edges just a bit." Ezra's hands clenched on the wheel. "I wouldn't. And he lives twenty miles from here. So don't worry."

Lacey offered a smile. "Maybe I'll short him a few slices of pepperoni."

Ezra grinned. "Now you're thinking. What if I do the delivery, and I deliver his last?"

Lacey said, "Don't clip the yellow lights. He'll be pacing and questioning why his pizza arrived in thirteen minutes instead of twelve."

"He'll always wonder if it was just coincidence that the mushrooms seemed to spell out 'JERK.'"

Lacey mused, "You've put far too much thought into ways to stick it to the customer."

Ezra sounded grim. "By the end of a long shift, you'll be thinking all these things, too."

Lacey snickered.

Ezra shrugged. "Anyhow, this order we're delivering, they're probably also wanting me to assemble a pie with the onions spelling out 'JERK' in beautiful script to send to the oven repair man who swore the heating element was fine and it's a safety feature when the oven turns off in the middle of preheating and then won't ever turn on again."

Lacey flinched. "While that would prevent a house fire, that also makes it difficult to roast a turkey."

"Yeah, given the monologue I got on the phone, I imagine twenty-two impending social media posts that Hartwell Appliance Repair is not number one on their recommendation list." Ezra slowed as he turned onto a side street. "Fortunately, it's Loveless Pizza to the rescue."

He had to ruin it. He must have forgotten he hated her while having a normal conversation, so then he had to say "Loveless" to annoy her again.

When they arrived, she carried the smaller bag while he hefted the larger one. A woman opened the door, shouting, "Dinner's here!" while a teen groaned, "Now everyone can shut up about the stupid oven," and then, through the chaos, a man was leading them to a kitchen where they could unload eight pizza boxes.

The man added, "You can set some of them on top of the stove, since there's no danger that they'll catch fire."

With a ripping sound, Ezra unsealed the hook-and-loop closure of the larger thermal bag and began stacking pizzas on the table. Lacey set her bag beside his and did the same.

"Ooh!" One of the guests bounded over holding a wine glass. "Look up! You're under the mistletoe!"

Someone shouted, "Now you have to kiss!"

Lacey froze.

Ezra glanced up, then said, "You get either kisses or pizza, but not both."

Lacey added, "And I assume you want the pizza."

A very sweet, very drunk guest began tapping her wine glass with a spoon. "Kisses! Everyone, they need to kiss!"

Another of the guests shouted, "Kiss her!" and Lacey shrunk. Ezra looked at her, very much on the alert. This was the expression on his face when he had three pies in the oven, one dough spinning in his hands, the computer chiming with an incoming order, and the phone ringing.

They were walled in by guests, and the woman who seemed to be the hostess said, "Well? You have to kiss her."

They were customers. They'd just bought eight pies and were highly likely to post on all their social media about the pizza shop that had saved the day with their clever Thanksgiving pizzas. You were supposed to give customers what they wanted. Ezra was claiming Lacey hadn't sacrificed a thing in her life, so she could make a sacrifice now. Just let him do it, and it would be over. It didn't have to mean a thing. They'd be just keeping the customers happy.

"Do it!" said one of the guests, and at least two cameras were up.

"We'll be customers for life," gushed the drunk woman, and someone else shouted, "Fifty dollar tip if you kiss!"

Lacey squared her shoulders. Turning to Ezra, she mouthed, "They're customers."

Ezra huffed. "Well. The customer is always right."

No. She didn't want the customer to be right. In fact, they were entirely wrong. But you do what you have to do.

The family started a chant: "Kiss! Kiss! Kiss! Kiss!"

Ezra declared in a loud voice, "My lady, may I take your hand?" and with her ears ringing, Lacey extended it.

Ezra bowed, then drew her hand toward him. She struggled not to yank it back. Then, when he had her fingers close to his lips, so near that his breath grazed against the small hairs on the back of her hand, he air-kissed, just shy of touching her skin.

There had to have been twenty pictures taken in two seconds while the family cheered, and that really drunk lady was banging on her wine glass again with her spoon.

Lacey's cheeks flamed, but Ezra dropped her hand and glanced at her like a conspirator.

Lacey clutched her almost-kissed hand to her throat. "Thank you, kind sir."

Ezra bowed to her again, then with steel in his expression, returned to unstacking pizzas.

What just happened?

Had he just protected her? They'd been walled in by cheering customers urging him to kiss her. He could have embraced her and planted his mouth on hers, and he could have justified forcing her by saying he'd had no choice. She'd technically given consent. He could have kissed her cheek and engulfed her in the wood-smokey scent of his hair and clothes, and then he could have blamed the mistletoe and the rules surrounding it all.

Lacey sat in the car holding a cash tip far in excess of anything they had a right to, including money shoved in her coat pocket by the very drunk woman who'd wished her an amazing life with her gorgeous husband.

Lacey fought herself not to look at Ezra, her "gorgeous husband." He had hair as red as hers, although not as red as her cheeks must be. They still felt hot. In his eyes, she must look like an idiot, and she still couldn't speak.

He probably did kiss well. But it would have been a kiss with someone who hated her. He could have humiliated her and later taunted her because she'd do anything for money. She'd sell pizza and sell her body, and it was all the same.

Except...he hadn't.

He wanted her gone. He didn't want her destroyed.

As they idled at a light, Ezra said, "How much did they tip?" His voice was subdued.

With trembling hands, Lacey counted the money in her lap. It was barely a tremble, so maybe Ezra didn't see it. "Sixty, and that one woman gave me an extra ten."

"I think she shoved money in my pocket, too, but I haven't checked." He chuckled. "It's too bad we don't work Christmas."

Lacey breathed, "Yeah, I was going to ask."

She hadn't been going to ask. It just made sense to keep her mouth moving so her brain didn't dial-tone.

He could have kissed her.

Knowing she hadn't truly consented, he'd...not done it.

He could have given her a kiss. Instead, he'd given her respect.

CHAPTER SIX

What had just happened?

As they pulled up at Loveless, Ezra kept thinking, *None of this went right.* Lacey shouldn't even be here, but Shelly should have been, and he shouldn't have been out on a delivery at all. The people who'd ordered eight pies should have had a working oven. They should have had better control over their guests, for that matter. Ezra should have threatened to call the cops or refused them delivery, except it had all happened so fast.

On Lacey's face had been an expression of fear. Fear, but resolve to kiss him if it meant keeping a customer happy. Half a second, and it would have been over, just a peck on the lips. No one would have demanded a romantic movie-ending embrace with the swell of violins in the background, and why not throw in a sunset why they were at it? Although it was Maine in November, so the sun was actually setting.

An air-kiss over her hand had been the only way out.

Except...for a moment, he'd had the impression Lacey would be really nice to kiss.

That was what left him shaken. Not the way customers could be dolts or the fact that they'd gotten a wad of cash in exchange for miming a kiss that hadn't taken place. No, it was the momentary way he'd taken leave of his senses and realized kissing her would feel amazing.

That was the woodsmoke talking. They'd worked together all day, and he'd forgotten for a moment how she wanted to destroy his pizzeria and his job and by extension his whole future. Talk about short-sighted.

Impulses weren't known for their long-term planning. That's why they got tamed.

Back inside, Lacey headed straight for the tip jar to shove in the wad of cash. She said to Shelly, "Are you doing better?"

Shelly had her head resting on crossed arms on the countertop. "Yeah, but you have an order. I told them forty minutes."

Ezra checked the oven temperature, then went to wash his hands. He took a long time doing it. Palms. Fingers. Back of the hand. Around the sides. Everything the way you learned when you got certified, except he was taking a lot more care than he needed to right now because behind him, Lacey kept making sure his sister was okay.

Why did Lacey care? Except maybe she did care?

All day, she'd been working hard for the pizzeria. Even Barrett hadn't started out that way. He'd certainly never delivered a pie further than the table where his buddies were camped out. At no point today had Lacey balked at any task, even the ugly parts. She'd washed equipment and scrubbed the stove top and sliced onions and roasted the turkey sausage.

Come to think of it, she'd never refused any job. The only times she'd hesitated were when she wasn't sure she could do it, not because it was gross. Never because it was beneath her.

With his hands rinsed and dried, Ezra returned to the counter. Shelly was holding out the order sheet. "Four pies, going to the police station. And before you ask, the order didn't come from the cops. Someone ordered it to be sent there, so we might get turned away at the door."

Ezra snorted. "Seriously?" and started tossing a dough.

Lacey said, "Did you charge their card yet?" When Shelly said she had, Lacey said, "Refund half of it. This part's on us."

Ezra fumbled the toss, wondering if the first time he dropped a dough would be right now, in front of Lacey. He caught it, though, and the act of tossing them helped steady his nerves. Lacey topped each pizza while he spread out the next, and then he slid them into the wood-fired oven. He felt hot, but he couldn't tell if it was heat from the work or heat from the near-kiss. What was the matter with him?

Why would he look at the instrument of his destruction and think, "Hey, she's kissable"? Or, "Hey, she's being nice to my sister and to the police department"?

Shelly told Lacey more about her trip into Hartwell with a dying car, and Lacey sounded horrified. Maybe she'd never driven for three months at a shot with the check engine light on, or changed her route because a dying transmission wouldn't make that one big hill. Ezra could fight the attraction by remembering exactly what he was dealing with: a rich girl, out of touch with reality, who thought of pizza as either a backup meal when your regular food went to heck (as if anyone could afford that?) or a "dining experience," and something to fancy up with organic this and locally sourced that.

The pizzas came out of the oven and into the boxes. Lacey stacked them in the thermal bag, but Shelly had already pulled on her jacket. "I can make this trip. Ezra, I'm taking your keys."

Lacey said, "Are you sure?"

"Yeah, gotta get back in the saddle." Shelly snorted. "Maybe my car will see me drive off in Ezra's and get jealous enough to fix itself," and then the door banged behind her.

Ezra really, really, really did not want Lacey to mention that near-kiss, so he preemptively changed the subject. "Why give the cops half off?"

"Emergency responders," Lacey said. "They're not only working a holiday, but they're probably handling the worst parts of humanity. Things like an angry drunk great-uncle throwing boiling gravy at his grand-niece because the potatoes weren't mashed enough."

Ezra snorted. "It's not a fun holiday until the cops show up. Then it gets really fun." He waved her over. "Wash your hands and come here."

When Lacey stepped up to the counter, he handed her a dough and the small wooden rolling pin. "First, make sure you've got plenty of semolina flour all over it." She set it on the counter and flipped it over. "Roll that to about ten inches in diameter."

Lacey's head tilted. Heaven help him, but she looked cute when she was puzzled. "You're going to make me do geometry? I never remembered radius and diameter and circumference." With the rolling pin over the dough, she hesitated. "This isn't going to be fit for human consumption."

"We call them Sunday Pies, because they're *holey*." Ezra warmed up inside when she groaned. "I always make a couple extra doughs, so you can ruin this if you want."

"You say *want* as though I have a choice." Lacey worked the rolling pin in a smooth motion, but slow. "My choice would be to keep rolling it in different directions, but when you roll, it's always in the same direction while you rotate the dough."

She'd been watching him? Ezra said, "You're doing fine."

When she had it about the right size, he said, "Now pick it up in your right hand, on your palm, and toss it up so you can catch it again."

She froze. "This is going to be a disaster."

Ezra shrugged. "It's just dough, and we won't sell out today anyhow."

She gave it a...well, not a toss. More like a jerk. The thing probably hadn't left her hand. Ezra said, "Lame."

"I'm going to destroy it." She did it again, and this time it at least got airborne, but it didn't spin.

Ezra said, "May I?" and rested his hand over hers to demonstrate. "Give it a little rotation." He gestured slowly, her wrist relaxing under his as he got her used to the motion. The rest of her was completely tense. "I'm serious about this. If you're going to own a pizzeria, you need to toss the dough."

Lacey gave it a reasonable toss, so it spun. She caught it, eyes bright with delight. "I did it!"

He grinned. "Do it a few more times."

"I'm a pizza goddess," she declared, and this time she

dropped it onto the counter. "Not much of a goddess. Not even an idol. Oh, well." She tried again. "Who came up with this? Why not roll it the whole way?"

Ezra said, "Tossing is faster, plus it makes the crust crustier. The inside gets thinner, and the outside doesn't. Now it's large enough to start catching it in two fists," he said. "Catch it so it drapes."

"All those words are English, but it sounds like you expect me to do that." She tried, and then laughed, but it wasn't a bad attempt. "I'm going to tear a hole in it."

"I already said, it's just dough." He waved her on. "Again."

She did it again with more confidence. As the dough grew, her hands naturally spread apart as she caught it, and finally she said, "When do I stop?"

"One more," he said, and then he had her lay it out on the counter.

She frowned at the misshapen circle. "You couldn't sell this."

"I've seen worse." When she didn't lighten up, he added, "It didn't hit the floor, so let's get it topped up."

Lacey snickered. "Someone's going to eat this?"

Ezra nodded "Of course."

"Pour soul." She spread the sauce, and then he topped it with cheese, onions, turkey sausage, and mushrooms. No orders had come in for a bit, so he waited until Shelly stepped back into the shop before shoving it into the oven.

Shelly unzipped her jacket. "The cops were surprised, but happy. I think they called an APB and made all units race back to the station to grab a slice."

Lacey said, "And anyone in the lockup?"

"Nah, those folks get to suffer with a mushy turkey

sandwich while the officers chow down in front of them. Or maybe not. It's not like they gave me a tour." She glanced at the oven. "Oh, good, another run."

Ezra said, "We're winding down. I may let the oven cool."

"Bummer." Shelly stretched. "Looks like you two raked in the tips today."

Lacey said, "You're still splitting tips. It's not your fault the car died."

Ah, right. The Rich Girl who could pass up perfectly good cash because...because she could.

At just the right moment, Ezra reached into the oven with the pizza peel and pulled out the bubbling pie, then set it directly on the counter. Four zips with the pizza cutter, and it was all set. "Dinner is served."

Lacey laughed. "I get to eat my own mistake?"

Shelly glanced at Ezra. "You let her make the pizza? You never let me make a pizza."

"She's about to own the place." That wasn't good enough for Shelly, though, so he added, "She needed to learn."

"Fine, fine." Shelly shook her head. "I'm letting that cool down by about two hundred degrees before I touch it, though."

While Ezra updated their social media to say they'd sold their last pizza for the day, Lacey set slices on paper plates and put a paper napkin to the left side of each. They ate at the counter, Ezra standing and Lacey and Shelly on the opposite side, on stools.

Ezra watched as Lacey took her first bite, and her eyebrows shot up. "Other than the crust, this is really good."

Ezra said, "So I still have a job?"

"Yeah, I can't replace you tomorrow."

Ezra teased, "We're closed tomorrow, so by Saturday...?"

Lacey crinkled her eyes at him. "Thanksgiving pizza sounded bizarre when you first said it, but it's a good idea."

Shelly said to Ezra, "That's two reasons you still have a job."

Ezra took a bite so he wouldn't have to reply.

Lacey said, "Fun innovations like this are why I want to expand what Lovelace offers."

Ezra swallowed quickly so he could say, "Please don't start that again."

Lacey said, "You can see you had a good idea. I'm *telling* you that this was a good idea—"

"And I'm telling you, it's a once a year thing." Ezra fought to keep his volume from rising. "We can't have fifty thousand toppings and a farmer with an ox cart at the back door—"

Shelly rubbed her hands together. "Oh, goodie—a fight! Just like the holidays at home."

Lacey said to Shelly, "He told me it's not a fun holiday until the cops show up, but then we showed up for the cops."

"No one's calling the cops, and it's *not* that kind of fight." Ezra glared back at Lacey. "We make good pizza. Everyone knows what they're getting. There's no reason to change."

Lacey didn't reply. No, why would she? After she took over, she could alter whatever she wanted at any moment, and his input wouldn't matter.

Regardless, the pizza was good. And Lacey still had that magnetic tug on him. Him, showing her how to toss pizza. How to roll it. How to get it into and out of the oven.

And her, looking as if she'd have let him kiss her.

None of it made, sense, so Ezra ate the pizza, and he tried not to think about her. Or at least, not think about her too much.

———◦———

Shelly didn't even wait for Ezra to turn on the engine. "Are you hot for her?"

The starter died, and Ezra recoiled. "What? Can you at least let me just drive you home without—"

"—without pointing out that you stare at her constantly?" The engine turned over this time. "I do not."

"Right, I didn't just watch your eyes boring into Lacey the entire time I was there." Shelly snickered. "Either you hate her or you love her, or maybe it's both, but seriously, the infatuation has got me rolling."

He didn't reply, so Shelly poked him with, "And you taught her to hand-toss a pizza?"

He pulled onto the road. "She has to learn."

"Did you wrap your arms around her and stand at her back, breathing into her ear, 'Here's where to put your hands to make it grow—'"

"Get your brain out of the gutter. If I touched her, the first thing she'd do is slap my hand."

Well, except she hadn't.

Shelly said, "You don't sound so sure about that."

"The delivery we did, the whole family was three sheets to the wind. They had mistletoe up."

Shelly bounced in the seat. "Did you kiss her?"

Ezra scowled. "They wanted me to."

Shelly prompted, "And?"

"And they went on about it! One lady, I thought she was going to slam me face-first into Lacey, so I did the only thing I could, and—"

61

"*Smoooooch*," Shelly drawled.

"If you'll let me finish, you pervert, I asked permission to take Lacey's hand—"

"You kissed her hand!" she crowed. "That is so romantic!"

"I stopped just short of kissing her hand, but the family thought it was a real kiss."

She collapsed back into the passenger seat. "Stop. I'm about to die here. That is the sweetest thing I've heard in a thousand years."

"And that's saying a lot, considering you're only twenty-one."

"You *air-kissed* her hand." Shelly shook her head. "I need to tell everyone I know, and they'll all line up for you. Except obviously you're taken." When Ezra snorted, she said, "Taken with Lacey. Your new owner."

"Stop right there. She'll own the shop. She won't own *me* any more than she'll own you."

Shelly steepled her fingers beneath her chin. "Except she'll own my big brother's big ole heart."

"Have you ever met us?"

"Your eyes were following her the whole time." Shelly grinned. "I know you hate her guts, but other than being a hellion who's intent on destroying your life, she's pretty nice. She looked out for me when I staggered in like a wounded rat. She even had me split tips even though I wasn't there for ninety-eight percent of the day."

Ezra didn't answer.

"Meanwhile, you hate her because she has *ideas*, but she hasn't implemented them. She talks about them, and you shut her down." Shelly shrugged. "I'd say, go along with her hairbrained notions, and then when they fail, be prepared to dial back and do what Loveless was doing before."

Ezra muttered, "Love-*lace.*"

"Yeah, that's just weird, but her name's *Lacey* so maybe she can't break the habit." Shelly snickered. "And maybe the next time you end up under the mistletoe, you'll want to take her in your arms for an actual kiss."

CHAPTER SEVEN

Lacey learned that December in a wood-fired pizzeria had an unexpected toastiness.

By the second week in December, Ezra still hated every single idea Lacey ever had, but she minded it less. If she had one thing to be thankful for, it was that she'd worked Thanksgiving Day and experienced Ezra for the first (and possibly only) time respecting her...respecting her as a human being, if not as the future owner.

In a matter of weeks, she'd learned a lot. She'd learned to maintain the oven temperature. She'd learned the trick to keeping a pizza peel clean but also keeping it functional. (Always use a dry rag.) She'd learned pizza terminology, too, such as "leopard spotting," which meant those delicious little black bubbles that rose on the crust when the oven was at its hottest. She learned that when Ezra portioned out the dough balls, he called it "doughnating." She also learned (after laughing) that he didn't consider it a joke.

Ezra was a good teacher. Without letting his dislike get in the way, he explained clearly and quickly, and he didn't mind when she took notes. Clarifying questions didn't exasperate him. Maybe because he had so many younger siblings, he'd developed a style of cutting to the chase. He'd explain to her one way, but then when a customer asked the same question, he'd explain in a different tone, using non-industry terms. He never sounded condescending. No, not even when a customer asked if cheese counted as a topping. (It didn't.) "How big is your sixteen inch pizza?" (Sixteen inches.)

Uncle Barrett turned up on occasion. It wasn't as often as Lacey would have figured, but Ezra at one point said, "Why's he around all the time?"

When Uncle Barrett worked with Ezra, the two men laughed. A lot. Sometimes they talked sports. Uncle Barrett would read back the comments on their social media posts, and he often shook his head about how "you young people" used slang, or outrageous customers' expectations.

The more she listened in, the more Lacey understood what customers liked about Lovelace Pizza, and she could imagine so many ways to build on those things.

Also, unfortunately, she understood what customers liked about Ezra. It wasn't just *"hot pizza made well and delivered fast."* His personality emerged in the social media quips. His humor sparkled even in the way he answered the phone. When he made a mistake (and it did happen, sometimes) he kept calm and eventually got the customer laughing. And finally, he looked genuinely hot working that wood-fired oven. It was embarrassing how often Lacey caught herself watching him as he worked in jeans, a black t-shirt, and that apron.

Second week of December, Lacey had an appointment. Uncle Barrett offered to work in the morning, declaring, "Me and Ezra, just like old times!"

Afterward, when she stepped in the door, Ezra and Uncle Barrett were mid-argument about the soccer game blaring from the TV. Uncle Barrett seemed to hold the side that the ref had made the stupidest call in the game, whereas Ezra insisted the ref had actually made the stupidest call in the entire worldwide history of soccer. Both men were at it full tilt.

With his back to her, Ezra was tossing pizzas, then setting them on the counter where Uncle Barrett could top them. Ezra never broke rhythm, not even while quoting statistics from last year's World Cup.

Lingering just inside the doorway, unseen, Lacey trained her eyes on Ezra in his element. Him and the warmth of the little building that was mostly kitchen. Him, keeping track of five things and yet never missing a cue. Orders came in on the phone or online, and pizzas came into and out of the oven, into boxes and then ready for delivery, and there were toppings to be monitored, as well as the occasional update to their social media. ("Only 20 pizzas left. Call soon because I want to go home.") Ezra turned on when he started work, and he didn't turn off again until afterward.

At least, Lacey assumed he turned off again afterward. Surely no one could maintain that intensity every hour of the day, every day of the week.

The other cook didn't work like this. Greg had less focus, more goofiness. He let more things slide.

Ezra turned to pull a pizza from the oven, and he caught sight of her.

His eyes widened, but then he was back in his zone, shoving the pizza peel under a finished pizza and sliding it into its box.

That little reaction caught her off guard. As he closed the box, he said, "Well, Barrett, it's over. Your replacement arrived."

Uncle Barrett laughed. "You're getting rid of the old man?"

Ezra returned to the oven to grab the next pizza. "You brought this on yourself. Can't complain if the person you're giving the pizzeria to actually goes ahead and takes over."

As Uncle Barrett unfastened his apron, Lacey said, "I believe the phrase is, 'hoist on your own petard.'"

"Never owned a petard. Never hoisted anything on one." Uncle Barrett tossed his apron in the bin. "Sliced with my own pizza wheel?"

Lacey started strapping on one of her own. "Topped with your own pepperoni?"

Ezra was ignoring them with such pointedness that he had to be listening. Lacey added, "Kneaded by your own Hobart?"

Uncle Barrett said, "That sounds painful," and then he left for the day.

Ezra boxed the second pizza, his eyes darker than usual, his mouth tighter. "Delivery."

Shelly wasn't delivering today. Lacey said, "You want me to do it?"

"We've got a driver, and I need you here," Ezra said. "We're behind, and you're faster than Barrett."

Lacey said, "At least I've got that going for me."

The next pizza was a pickup, and Ezra stashed that on

top of the oven. Their delivery driver arrived and left again. An order came in for two meat lover pizzas, so Ezra got to work.

"You're faster than he is," Ezra had said. For all that he'd sounded bitter when saying, "You brought this on yourself," this admission hadn't sounded begrudging. Lacey was faster. Uncle Barrett was more fun to be around. Or was he just more permissive?

Or was Ezra bitter because no one would have demanded he kiss Uncle Barrett's hand?

Regardless, Ezra was fastest, and two meat lover pizzas got laid out at record speed.

The pickup customer arrived. Lacey took care of him at the register, and when she turned to him with the total, he had one of the boxes open. "This is unacceptable."

Ezra wasn't looking up, but again, Lacey could tell he was paying attention. She said, "That's what you ordered."

Even as she spoke, Lacey took an inventory of the toppings. It was fine.

The man said, "There's not enough meatballs. If I'm paying for a meat lover pizza, I expect meat. A lot of meat. And the crust is burnt."

That pizza was fine. Before Lacey could say anything, the man yanked up a slice, and toppings slid off. "Look at this! It's a mess! And it's soggy! Your cook over there is incompetent."

Lacey repeated, "To be clear, you're saying he made it wrong?"

Ezra glared at her, but come on, this was a freebie-seeker. In the next sentence, the guy was going to either ask for a full refund, or else he was going to demand that second pie for free. Or maybe he was a seasoned grifter who'd demand she fire Ezra and then back down and settle for her only comping this and giving him coupons for the next order.

The man glared at Ezra. "Look at him. He doesn't even care."

Lacey lifted both boxes off the counter without even closing the lid, leaving the customer standing with the bottom of the slice he'd yanked out—the cheese and toppings having remained with the pizza.

The customer exclaimed, "What are you doing?"

Lacey walked the pizzas to the back counter. "They're not up to your standards. We can't disappoint you." Ezra looked livid, probably thinking she was going to force him to remake them, but she ignored him as she smiled at the customer. "You may find a better meat lover pizza over at Jake's Pizza up the road, or House of Pizza on the other side of Hartwell."

Ezra straightened.

The man exclaimed, "What? You're not going to serve me?"

Lacey opened her hands. "You're the one who refused service, not us."

Ezra returned to tossing a pizza, smirking. The customer said, "Listen, little lady, I want to talk to your manager."

Organic locally-sourced sexism: Lacey's favorite. "I'm the manager."

The man clenched his fists and pulled himself up taller. "You can't deny me a pizza. Give them back."

Lacey lowered her pitch a little. "You were disappointed that there weren't enough toppings on the pizza, and you were also upset that the pizza had too many toppings. You claimed it was too soggy *and* it was too burnt. There's no way we can meet all your expectations. Try Jake's."

It wouldn't surprise her if this man had already worn out his welcome with both Jake and Hartwell House of Pizza.

The man pointed to the boxes. "Make it right. Fifty percent off."

Would money dry up the sogginess and de-crisp the crispiness and spontaneously generate an extra meatball? "Ezra's a master pizza-maker, and that pizza is perfect. I have never seen him make a single one of the mistakes you just accused him of, let alone all of them at the same time."

Ezra nearly dropped the dough he was tossing, and he didn't start again.

The customer snorted. "You're new here, sweetheart, but he screws up every time. He shorts the toppings, and the pizza gets burnt. I only came tonight because I thought I'd get the other guy."

"The other guy" being Greg, or being Uncle Barrett? Lacey said, "Ezra has never screwed up a pizza. The first pizza he made was perfect, and the last pizza he ever makes will also be perfect."

Ezra still hadn't moved.

The customer jabbed a finger toward the pizzas. "Give them to me, and I want them for free."

Lacey tilted her head. "You can leave. You're now banned from ordering from us again."

The man spat out, "I know the owner!"

Lacey shrugged. "So do I."

The man flung the naked slice of pizza onto the floor, then stepped toward the edge of the counter as if he were going to come after her. Lacey backed up.

Ezra spoke for the first time. "Don't."

It was a low tone, a threatening note. Ezra had squared

his shoulders and was staring the customer dead in the eye. Not a muscle moved, but he'd set his jaw, and his eyes had a black glint of fury.

Although he wasn't holding a weapon, Ezra looked like the deadliest man in creation. Behind him, the wood-fired stove smoldered, and before him, the customer breathed unsteadily.

The man growled, "You're losing a customer."

"Customers are people who spend money." Ezra's eyes narrowed. "So far, you haven't."

In a situation about to explode, Ezra stood firm, rock-solid. He was capable of anything. The same man who'd taken Lacey's fingertips and brushed near them without touching stood beside her like unexploded ordinance, and he was ready for everything.

The man swept the napkin holder off the counter and shouted, "I'm getting you all fired," but he started moving toward the exit. "I'm writing reviews everywhere. I'm telling them what you're really like."

He hit the glass door with his fist, but it didn't shatter. He tried to slam the door at his back, too, but then the safety release caught, so it closed with a sweet slowness.

That failed door-slam should have been funny. Lacey should have wanted to laugh. Instead, only then did she realize how hard it was to breathe.

With a huff, Ezra punched a button on the screen to bring up the next order.

"Thank you," Lacey murmured.

Her voice didn't need to be that low. It wasn't as if the customer was coming back.

Ezra's voice was equally low. "Barrett would have given him both pies for free."

She started. "Wait—should I—?"

"Barrett collapses like a house of cards. Customers will blame me for nothing, and he'll comp the whole order." Ezra glanced at Lacey. "At least you don't have the spine of a jellyfish."

He looked almost pleasant, almost as if he could tolerate her. She had one quality he could approve of. She ought to grab that and run.

Lacey crinkled her eyes at him. "And here I thought you'd get angry that I'm ruining the business by annoying the customers."

"Some customers cost more than they bring in." He hesitated. "You didn't have to lie for me."

Lacey straightened. "When did I lie?"

"That you think I'm good at my job. I know it's a customer service thing, but—"

Lacey exclaimed, "You *are* good at your job."

Ezra rolled his eyes. "Listen, we both know you think I have no idea what I'm doing."

"How did I give you that impression?" Lacey's heart pounded. "You're amazing when you've got everything going all at the same time, keeping track of the pizzas in the oven and the pizzas you're topping and the orders that have already come in and predicting the new orders about to arrive, not to mention tracking how many pizzas we have left in the day."

Ezra fixed her with the same look he'd given the irate customer, and like him, Lacey stopped in her tracks. He said, "I'm not fishing for compliments. But I'm also not looking for you to go on a PR campaign with irrational people. Barrett always agrees with them. *Yeah, Ezra mucked it up again, have a freebie.*"

"But you *didn't* muck it up, and I have never seen you muck anything up." Her eyes stung. "What gave you the idea that I think you're incompetent?"

Ezra said, "Nothing I do is good enough for you."

Her heart stuttered. "Nothing?"

He swept out an arm to take in the place. "Nothing. You didn't even know the shop yet when you decided to change everything, and when I tell you something's not going to work, you ignore every word I say. I'm going to walk in one day to find a cow in my parking spot and you milking it—"

She raised her hands. "I'm not talking about milking cows. When it comes to making pizzas, you are the best there is. You don't make mistakes—at least, none I've seen."

Ezra tilted his head.

Lacey said, "You're top notch at the pizza part. But that doesn't mean you know the back end of the business."

Ezra opened his hands. "And see? Right there, you ruin it. You could have left it at, *No, man, you're good,* and we'd be fine. But even after working here since the day Loveless opened its doors, to your mind, I still don't know how anything works. I'm a trained monkey who spreads sauce and throws wood into the oven."

Lacey huffed. "Yes, that's exactly what I said. A monkey with safety certification and a social media account."

Ezra gave her a thumbs up as he returned to work. "Thanks. I appreciate it."

"While you're listing the people nothing's good enough for, go ahead and add yourself to that list, because you've shot down every idea I've had since the moment Uncle Barrett walked me in the door."

Ezra snapped, "Because you won't give the place a

chance."

Lacey shot back, "At what point did you give me a chance?"

He faced her. "A chance to do what? To destroy the business?"

"To make it succeed!" She stepped toward him. "You wrote me off from minute number one as a nepotism brat with no experience and no credentials, and you've got nothing to say except change is impossible."

"The changes you want to make are dumb." He folded his arms. "They're performative, and they're nothing our customers would ever be interested in."

Lacey said, "Then I want to know what changes you think they *would* be interested in."

"Nothing!" His eyes blazed. "They think everything's fine as it is. They want to call us for a hot pizza and have it on the table in twenty minutes."

Lacey said, "And if we don't change a few things, they're going to call us for a pizza and have nothing on the table because we're going to close."

CHAPTER EIGHT

So...things were a lot worse than Ezra ever thought.

"I should have known," he muttered as he drove home. Barrett had the business sense of a naked mole rat, and after winning a pizzeria in a poker game, he'd opened for business because it seemed like fun to own a pizza joint. He'd retired from his career—which he'd planned to do anyhow—and played "restaurateur" with Loveless.

What he hadn't done was taken a salary.

Barrett, as the owner, had sometimes split tips with Ezra (always with a delighted look in his eye, like a preschooler fishing loose change out of a Christmas stocking) but Ezra never realized Barrett hadn't been paying himself. He'd lived on his retirement income or disbursals from a 401K or a pension or whatever funds could afford three properties and poker nights where tipsy old men wagered a defunct business on a full house.

Now that the fun had worn off, Barrett was giving it away, but whoever got it wasn't going to be an old retired man with stars in his eyes. The new owner would want an income. And the money wasn't there.

The vendors got paid. The two employees got paid. The delivery drivers got paid, plus tips. And the new owner... would have to get rid of one of the two employees if she wanted to survive.

Greg was part-time, so that left one candidate.

Ezra slammed his fist into the dashboard. He should have known. Should have known, should have known, should have known. This gig was too good to be true. He'd taken it because it was a way to get first and last month's rent and a security deposit on a room in a house in a tiny town in Maine before the gig flamed out harder than the logs in the wood-fired pizza oven. It was a way to sleep in a bed and a way to send money back to a trailer home where his siblings were crammed in like sardines.

He'd gotten three years out of this three-month bad-idea-fueled gig. He should count his blessings, but for crying out loud—this job was fun. He'd grown to like Hartwell. He liked his customers. (Well, the drunk mistletoe-fans aside. And the scammers. But the rest were fine.)

Lacey hadn't said anything about the money when she'd plotted all these changes. She'd said it would be good for the community to have farm-to-table organic produce that didn't even realize it had been harvested yet, and mozzarella where you could drive past the cow who'd made the milk that morning. Lacey hadn't said, "If I don't do this, I'm going to have to fire you," which wouldn't have made her ideas any less dumb, but it would have given her meddling a different spin.

When she'd been changing things for the sake of

changing them—putting her cute little stamp on them—that was reckless and arrogant. Changing things because only a course-correction would stave off bankruptcy was different. It was desperate.

Christmas was coming, and she hadn't wanted him worried. But he wasn't a child.

Typical rich girl. It never occurred to her that maybe he'd need to save money now if he was going to be unemployed for a while.

Shelly had other delivery gigs, so closing wouldn't cause trouble for her. She'd pick up extra hours somewhere else. He should tell Greg. Or maybe he shouldn't because Greg had all the forward planning skills of a golden retriever, and telling Greg to prepare for his job to end would likely result in Greg saying, "Nah, it'll be fine." Which, somehow, it always ended up being for Greg.

Ezra had never been that lucky.

Lacey's voice had been strained. "Uncle Barrett never took a salary. I looked over all the records, though, and I think we've got a chance. But what are the options? We can't jack up the prices. I don't want anyone fired. I won't lower salaries. I can't live without money. That's why we need to shake things up."

Ezra had said, "Why would you even take over the place if that's how it is?"

She'd lowered her voice, "I knew we could expand it. Increase the number of pizzas per day. Increase the offerings. Reach out to the organic and whole foods customers."

Every one of which, Ezra had shot down.

Ezra had told her, "Those things wouldn't have worked."

Lacey had replied, "You won't hear me out about finding

a cheaper supplier."

"Because the quality has to be good." Ezra had turned away. "You can't cut quality and increase the price and expect the customers to stick around. We really will close."

Lacey had said, "You want everything to stay the same. I can't make the necessary changes without making any changes."

He'd hated her. She'd come in with guns blazing, waiting for the day Barrett handed her the keys so she could obliterate everything that made Loveless unique in a town with plenty of pizza options. That had been easy to accept: she was self-important. Except as it turned out, he couldn't hate what she was trying to achieve.

Lacey had said, "There's nothing to hide. I'll show you the accounts."

Barrett had never done that. The business had account numbers on file with all their suppliers, and once a week, Ezra's bank account got an electronic transfer. At the end of the day, Ezra and anyone else who'd worked would sort out the cash tips while a program automatically divided up the electronic ones. With the system paying out seamlessly, Ezra had never wondered how much remained in the bank afterward.

Lacey had trembled, eyes sad and hands open at her side, looking right at him as she said, "If you think none of my ideas will work, that's fine. But we need to try something. This business can't afford to pay you and me and Greg and Shelly."

"Barrett had no idea what he was doing," Ezra said to the dashboard, but he'd said it first to Lacey, standing there with the wood-fired oven at his back and two orders arriving on the online system. "I knew he was paying me more than market. But I was opening a restaurant. I thought—"

...and then for Barrett to give it to Lacey...

I thought it would have been me.

Lacey had said to him, "What did you think?"

Ezra had turned to the counter.

And she'd said—

He stopped at a red light.

—she'd said, "You thought he was going to sell it to you?"

Ezra closed his eyes and breathed deeply. No, he hadn't thought about it that way. But even though Barrett was retirement age, he was young-ish. He didn't *do* anything for Loveless, so Ezra had assumed he'd just continue doing nothing for another twenty years. And yeah, maybe in twenty years, Ezra might have been able to take it over. Twenty years of counting every penny, living in a back room in a house with random roommates and a car he was never sure would make it through the winter. Twenty years of sending money back home, except as the kids grew up, he'd be able to send less and save more.

Lacey's voice had gone soft, "I didn't know any of this. Uncle Barrett only said you were vital."

She'd looked as broken as he felt, but he'd only squared his jaw and prepared the next pizza so he couldn't see her sadness. She'd asked for suggestions, but he had none. She was right that things had to change even though he wanted nothing to change. She'd been right all along. And if she'd been right about that, then maybe she was right that he'd never given her a chance, and maybe she was right that he'd treated her unfairly.

Maybe there'd been more to her from the start.

The light turned green. Driving again, Ezra said, "And

that was it, Mr. Lovelace. You were pretending to work, like Marie Antoinette putting on peasant garb and milking a cow, play-acting at being one of the working class. But it was never real to you. Not like it was to me."

For the last few years, pizza was reality. It was substance, and it was food. Pizza was what you got when you moved and started over. It was what you got when someone died and you struggled to process the end. It was quick and cheap and filling. It was carbs and fat and protein, and anything the base didn't provide, you could get in the toppings. It was comfort and sameness, and also there was just enough variation to keep it interesting. Interaction after interaction with the customers had convinced Ezra that pizza and life were the same.

After one conversation with Lacey, he knew it had all been a game of pretend.

———◦———

Ezra showered before bed, then scrolled social media. The Loveless Pizza page had its usual assortment of comments. It would be a shame if the place closed even though they had a healthy number of regulars.

He texted Lacey, "What about premium pizzas?"

Her reply came momentarily. "I'm listening."

"I still think farm-to-table would be a disaster, but Loveless thrives on limited supply. What if we introduce customers to the idea by having a premium pizza that's only available at certain times. We charge more, but it's very limited."

"Like Thanksgiving pizzas?"

He replied, "I guess."

She texted, "So for the rest of December, we offer ten mistletoe pizzas per day?"

Ezra frowned. "Isn't mistletoe poisonous?"

"I'm sure it would taste terrible, too. But let's say you make them. How much extra could we possibly charge that would keep the business afloat?"

She had a point. He texted, "We probably can't add gold leaf to the pizza."

She sent a goofy emoji face. "Most restaurant suppliers are fresh out of gold leaf this time of year."

Ezra texted, "Mine-to-table," before thinking maybe he shouldn't, but Lacey replied with a laughing emoji.

She sent, "I know you don't want to change the cap on how many doughs we do per day, but what if we made it 100 regular orders, and 20 of the premium?"

He frowned at the phone. That might actually work.

She continued, "That would keep 'the Loveless One Hundred,' but it would also spur the fear of missing out."

He texted, "Does each mistletoe pizza come with a serial number?"

She replied, "I'll bring a permanent marker, and we can write it on the box."

He replied, "That's great, but what goes on a mistletoe pizza?" Then added, "Since mistletoe is poison."

She replied, "I just checked, and American mistletoe won't kill you. It'll only make you extremely sick."

He texted, "Which won't sell many pizzas," and immediately her text came with, "I guess that's not a great endorsement."

After a pause, she sent, "We could put a tiny breadstick under each slice so when you pull it out, it's Christmas tree shaped."

He typed, "Unworkable," before stopping himself. She'd already accused him of shooting down all her ideas (poisonous toppings aside) and this idea wasn't as awful as some of her others, so he deleted the text. Finally, he sent, "It has to be more than shape."

What would he put on a holiday-themed pizza? Typical "winter" flavors didn't work on a pizza. Peppermint, eggnog, cinnamon: no. Ooh, gingerbread! Another no.

She texted, "Let's play with shapes for a minute. Could we claim round slices of fresh mozzarella are snowballs?"

He blinked at the phone. Finally, he replied, "What about slices of tomato with a sprig of basil behind, so they look like Christmas balls?"

She replied, "Wait, we could do party-sized wreath pizzas. The outside has a cornucopia of toppings, and the inside is plain, and we slice it in a party cut."

He replied, "Different sizes would cause logistical problems."

She replied, "Rats."

They could do it regular size, though. It wouldn't have the same impact as, say, a 24 inch pizza, but it could be done.

A minute later, she'd texted a terrible sketch: a long triangle he assumed was a pizza slice, and laid out on the slice were three circles and a lumpy triangle on top. Pointing to each of the three circles were the words, "onion," "tomato slice," "mozzarella slice," and to the lumpy triangle, "mushroom hat."

Accompanying the photo were the words, "Snowman slice."

Ezra replied, "I'm not sure if this is ridiculous or brilliant."

"Could be both, but for now, let's go with brilliant."

He replied, "Fine, a brilliant mistletoe pizza."

The screen indicated she was typing, and then nothing showed up. Finally, "Thank you."

Five minutes for "Thank you." He replied, "For what?"

She sent, "For brainstorming."

He texted, "There's got to be a way out of this."

Right now, Ezra could see only one way out. The only way for Loveless to survive was for Ezra to quit.

CHAPTER NINE

Ezra had better not quit. He'd looked ready to walk out the door, and that's when she'd blurted out their financial problems.

It wasn't fair to dump that on him. Not right before Christmas.

The thing was, Lacey could make it function if she just... didn't work there. The pizzeria seemed like a self-sustaining operation, except that was all it did. It could keep churning out a limited number of pizzas and paying its bills forever and ever and ever, but in order to do more than cover its own operating costs, it needed to grow.

Ezra's eyes had been fire. She'd never seen him like that before—first his fury at the customer, but then his fury at her. And then he'd shut down.

So for him to reach back out to her about premium pizzas? That meant everything. She'd kept her mouth shut at first about how he was rearranging the deck chairs on the Titanic, but then when she'd asked questions, he'd actually budged a little. Maybe they could do more than a hundred doughs a day. Maybe—for the premiums—they could expand a bit. He'd still keep his sacred *Loveless one hundred* intact. But at the same time, they'd bring in more income.

That said, she needed a better name than "mistletoe pizza," due to the aforementioned "makes you wretchedly ill" problem. Her snowman pizza was desperately cute, and (she got the impression) desperately what Ezra wanted not to do.

On the other hand, they were talking.

In the end, they went with the Wreath Pizza: an assortment of toppings in a ring inside the crust, plain cheese on the inside, and an optional party pizza cut.

Ezra announced it on the website, but first he teased it. "We're only making five," he posted on a Thursday. "If they don't sell, we're never making another, so you'll want to grab one while you can."

They sold all five in an hour. On Friday, Ezra posted, "Fine. We'll up it to ten, just to see. Order a party cut for tonight's hockey game."

It worked. Not only did it work, but people who ordered a Wreath Pizza inevitably ordered other things as well, so they sold out the Loveless one hundred earlier than usual.

Then, Sunday. Both the Patriots and the Bruins were playing. "Six thirty and we're down to the final twenty?" Lacey exclaimed.

Looking unsurprised, Ezra said, "I figured we would. Two games, Sunday night, getting on toward Christmas— no one's going outside. Combine Christmas parties and football parties, plus people who just got back from shopping and don't feel like cooking." He chuckled. "I like these nights."

Lacey huffed. "That cap means we're leaving money on the table."

Ezra stiffened. She said, "You predicted we'd run out early. We could have prepped more doughs and sold more."

He said, "We're still operating under Barrett's rules. Yes, even though you're doing the premiums—"

Lacey said, "And we need to brainstorm another premium, because those are fun."

"—I know, they're fun," Ezra snapped, "but how many pizzas do you think we'd have to sell per day to keep your rent paid?"

She snapped, "And it's totally unreasonable for me to expect to get a living wage? Or are you just comfortable getting paid for doing nothing?"

With an expansive sweep of his arms, he exclaimed, "Doing nothing?"

"Yes! When we sell out two hours early, that's paying you for doing nothing." Her eyes narrowed. "My uncle had no business sense. We agree on that. You're taking advantage."

He folded his arms. "So operating under the terms of my employment agreement is taking advantage? Or is it taking advantage to bamboozle your uncle into giving you a pizzeria?"

She stalked into the storage room to breathe before she started yelling.

At her previous restaurant job, some wag had put up a sign (she hoped it wasn't management) saying, "Employees must stop crying before exiting the walk-in." In a busy kitchen, you couldn't get space to break down after a customer screamed at you or a line cook pinched your body or the manager questioned your ability to think at higher than a third grade level. The employee bathroom was generally disgusting, so for a quiet sob, that left the walk-in.

She didn't need to cry, but she did need to get a break from Ezra's onslaught.

Working for six weeks was the test to see whether she'd even want to complete the deal. Ezra was part of the deal, though, and Ezra was the single factor making it impossible to move forward. She could bail on the deal and ask Uncle Barrett for the trust fund instead. Heaven knew he'd get money if he sold Lovelace. For that matter, he could just keep Lovelace Pizza and never interact with it again while it treaded water. At least...until the minute the boiler broke, or they needed a new oven. Any unexpected expense would tank the place.

The trouble with treading water was, you never got anywhere. Treading water was never supposed to be a long term solution. It just kept you in place until you could be safe again.

A shadow in the door. Ezra, who never gave up on anything, leaned in the door frame. "You do have the right to change the terms of my employment. You can force me to make a hundred twenty pizzas a day. You can force me to make zero."

Her voice was unsteady. "I'm not forcing you out, and I wish you'd do me the same courtesy."

He said, "I can't force you out."

"You could make working here awful enough that I walk. But no one else is going to take over this business without making the same changes I'm suggesting, so you should probably stop making me miserable."

He didn't reply.

She wrapped her arms around herself and took a deep breath. The other reason to cry in a walk-in was the chill. The frozen air brought you back to yourself because cold lit up all your nerves. Especially in Maine, cold was an ever-present threat, lurking even in the summertime. The land didn't want humans here, the same way Ezra didn't want her here. But the chill—the startling nature of frost—brought you back to yourself. You'd stop crying and then go back to getting the job done.

When finally he spoke, all Ezra said was, "I wish Barrett weren't doing this."

Lacey swallowed hard. "I understand. No matter what changes, you lose."

Life never let you stay the same. Bills needed to be paid. Old men got older and wanted to retire for real.

Ezra said, "I was living in my car. I don't want to go back to that."

Lacey blinked hard, looking aside so he wouldn't see if tears came to her eyes. "I'm sorry. Sorry you were living in your car, that is. But you'll forgive me if I don't think I should have to live in mine."

The computer chimed with an incoming order, so Lacey started walking out of the supply room. Ezra caught her arm, and she turned to him.

He was gazing right in her eyes. So tall. He smelled of wood smoke and pizza sauce, and she got caught up in the aura of him, his hand on her shoulder, his eyes dark in the shadows of the storage room. She didn't bother hiding her eyes now. She wasn't crying. She just wished they'd quit fighting.

He said, "I don't want you miserable."

She said, "When you cooperate with me, we actually work like a team."

He didn't release his grip. "You want me on your team?"

Lacey blurted out, "What if you and I were on the same side? What if we worked together instead of against one another?" Ezra recoiled, and she moved closer. "You make excellent pizza, but you also make good decisions. You make the best with what you have. You look out for the people you love. You stand up for what you believe in. Yes, I would love to have you on my team."

He rested his hand on her other shoulder. She tilted her face toward him, and he kissed her.

She knew the instant he did it that they shouldn't be kissing—that it was all wrong to kiss the man who was about to become her employee, and that this changed nothing—and therefore, she didn't stop. Because after she stopped, she'd have to never do it again.

Yes, she wanted him on her team—but she'd also come to admire him. And here he was, just him and her in a dark room in a little building and a huge question—and a lot of tremendous feelings swirling. They could make this work. This—the pizzeria, the partnership, maybe friendship. But nothing more. Kissing him was a huge mistake. She needed to back off.

Instead, she put her hand behind his neck while he slipped one of his hands to the base of her back and tugged her toward him. He wasn't urgent, not as if he was devouring her and her dreams and future success. He could be strong when he wanted, forceful and powerful, but to her, wrapping his arms around her waist and running his lips across her jaw, he was gentle.

She choked out, "We should stop."

He breathed into her ear, "I know," and then he had his mouth again on hers.

They shouldn't be kissing. She shouldn't have one hand knotted in the strap of his apron, and she shouldn't have her eyes closed as he kissed her throat down to her shoulder. She shouldn't run one hand through his hair, and she certainly shouldn't have grabbed him when he pulled away and then kissed him again.

When he paused, clutching her tightly, he sagged against the door frame. "Am I about to get fired?"

She rested her head against his collar bone, feeling his breath heaving against her cheek. "Well...I did ask you to brainstorm." When he choked out a laugh, she said, "No ideas are bad ideas, so—"

Then he was kissing her again, this time more urgent. She pressed against him—and Shelly's car door thunked outside.

They separated like a pair of cats under the garden hose. Lacey fled out to the computer to grab the most recent order. As Shelly entered, Ezra exited the back room holding a can of tomato sauce.

Lacey said, "Two pies, one veggie, one wreath." Did her voice wobble?

Ezra headed to the hand-washing station as though thirty seconds ago they hadn't been all over one another.

Shelly stripped off her jacket, saying, "Wow, it's hot in here!"

Ezra only said, "You think so?" and despite the wood-fired oven, that really made Lacey shiver.

———◦———

Ezra couldn't take his eyes off Lacey.

Every bewitching move of hers hooked him further into her world. He wanted to touch the strands of red hair that had escaped their binding and framed her face, and when she had a smudge of flour on her chin, he hungered to kiss it off.

Thank goodness Shelly was here, awaiting the next delivery.

Two people loving the same thing should not mean those two people would love each other. They were united for a cause, not for a lifetime. Lacey loved a pizzeria, not him. He loved the same pizzeria, but that didn't justify clutching her body against his and losing himself in the sensation of her.

Make pizza, not romance. *Loveless* pizza. That was the key. Loveless.

Except— Dang, Lacey was amazing.

Of course, now she was also skittish, so Ezra tried to hide the way he wanted to stare at her. She shouldn't see it. Especially neither should Shelly, who still mocked him for air-kissing Lacey's hand.

He could have had that first kiss weeks ago. What was he thinking? Oh, right, he was thinking that Lacey hadn't wanted a kiss, and therefore, a kiss was not to be given.

An order came in for delivery. Which, unfortunately, meant Shelly would be out the door in ten minutes. Trying to figure out what to do, Ezra tossed another dough while Lacey began dressing the pizza.

Lacey said aloud, "I think I just made a mistake."

He glanced at her, but she was only spreading the sauce. It didn't look like a mistake. Ezra said, "It looks okay to me."

Lacey said, "From my angle, it looks different."

Oh. Got it.

Ezra said, "You think you added too much, too soon?"

Lacey sounded unnerved. "Yeah."

From the counter, without looking up from her phone, Shelly said, "It's just a pizza. No one's going to notice."

Lacey said, "But once you see something, it's hard not to keep seeing it."

Ezra said, "You can probably cover for it. Like, if you know something happened once, you can make sure it doesn't happen again."

Even if you want it to. Scratch that: especially if you want it to.

Lacey started spreading cheese. "You think it's possible to cover over a mistake like that?"

Ezra said, "We're in a pizzeria. Ninety seconds at eight hundred degrees. That mistake will be gone, and no one will see it again."

Lacey added, "Because I'd hate to ruin everything."

Shelly looked up. "You're getting a little dramatic. The worst that can happen with a real mistake is the customer gets annoyed, and you offer them a free pizza."

What was the equivalent of comping a passionate kiss? Ezra couldn't just pay Lacey off and say, *"Sorry, babe, the next one's on me."* Lacey was saying, without saying, that the minute Shelly stepped out the door with the new pizzas was not the minute Lacey stepped back into Ezra's embrace.

So Ezra said, "You don't want to lose a customer, though."

Lacey said, "Especially an important customer."

Ezra said, "That's why we treat the business like professionals."

Lacey's shoulders relaxed as she reached for the black olives. "Okay. As long as one mistake won't ruin everything."

Ezra nodded. "Exactly. Pizza's comfort food, but we don't need to involve anyone's emotions."

He hated that, but they needed to get back on track. She wanted Loveless to succeed, and right now everything depended on working as a team.

Teamwork meant sacrifice. He could sacrifice a relationship before it began. For the sake of the pizzeria, that sacrifice would be necessary.

Although, come to think of it, a larger sacrifice might be necessary. Because all Lacey's problems could be solved with one simple move—one Lacey had so far refused to make.

Ezra could do it for her, and then it would all be resolved.

Loveless couldn't afford to pay full-time salaries for both him and her. He'd proven one full-timer was enough to keep the place going, though. The money would suffice if Ezra stepped aside.

He hated it, but it was the only way out for her. And then she could make all the changes she wanted.

Shelly set down her phone. "You guys are making it sound like the world's ending, but it's just pizza. Pizza is salty enough without adding tears."

Lacey moved to start on the second dough. "Makes sense. The only broken hearts should be the Loveless pizzas—and those aren't until Valentine's Day."

By then, Ezra wouldn't be working here any longer.

CHAPTER TEN

Lacey checked the computer calendar on Saturday morning. "Welcome to the last Saturday before Christmas!" she called. "It's a no-customers day!"

Today would be easy-easy-easy. They had one client who'd ordered seventy-five pizzas to be delivered throughout the day.

The Hobart was running, and Ezra called from the supply room, "I hope you're ready for a nice, slow day."

He'd behaved himself for the past week, which was good because it meant Lacey had been behaving herself, too. Gosh, it was tough making sure she never touched him, never got too close again. He moved like a lynx, his eyes like a predator's but also gleaming with strength. He saw everything. Every so often, she thought she caught him seeing right through her.

She did not need another complication. If she got emotionally involved, she'd never keep the business afloat. Loveless Pizza required level-headed decisions, not urgent kisses in the storage room.

Speaking of which, she said to Ezra, "Once the slow day is over, I have something to run past you about the business."

He paused, looking pained. "Yeah. I need to talk to you about that, too."

Well, that sounded ominous. But she didn't need a complication right at the day's beginning, so she shoved the thought out of her head.

Lacey checked out the calendar on the office desk, marked in Barrett's handwriting with "Castleton Music School," with deliveries to start at noon. It was just the one customer today, and Shelly to make the deliveries. Greg had scrawled his days in the shop across Friday and Sunday, and Ezra had marked Monday as a supply delivery day. All was well.

Lacey's phone rang, and it was Uncle Barrett. He said, "Lacey, I hope you don't mind, but I have a last minute order."

Lacey went to stand in the doorway. "You're saying we don't get a quiet day here after all?"

Ezra looked up at her.

Uncle Barrett said, "I know, you were only going to do sixty doughs, but I've got another order for forty."

It was seventy-five, Lacey thought. Another forty would put them over Ezra's cap, but he wouldn't gripe about the actual owner making that decision.

Uncle Barrett continued, "The country club had a kitchen fire last night, but today is their biggest fund-raiser of the year. It's for childhood cancer research, so I volunteered us. I'll cover the cost myself."

Lacey said to Ezra, "We're doing another forty," and he

rolled his eyes. She returned her attention to the phone. "Sure, that only brings us to a hundred fifteen. Was anyone hurt?"

Ezra stepped closer, and she said, "Kitchen fire at the country club. They need us to save the day."

He posed like a super hero, which was both funny and more than a little tempting, so Lacey gave a nervous laugh and turned away to keep talking to Uncle Barrett. "What time do they need us to start delivering?"

Uncle Barrett said, "No one was hurt, only equipment. Deliveries should start at two o'clock."

Lacey said, "Sure, let the high class donors slum with pizza."

Ezra muttered, "Probably the realest thing they'll deal with all year," and Lacey smirked at him.

Uncle Barrett gave her the rest of the details, which she jotted on the desk calendar alongside his original note. They shouldn't need to call in Greg for this, although they might need an extra driver if they were going in two directions at once.

Ezra had begun doughnating individual dough balls out of the Hobart, so Lacey said, "I'll update our social media and tell people where they can go to get more pizza," and then, a minute later, she chuckled. "You've got a mistake here. Should I fix it?"

When she faced Ezra, once again she had the impression he'd been checking her out. Good luck with that, though. She'd wrapped on her apron and tucked up her hair in the hair net. He said, "What's the mistake?"

"You posted that we're delivering pizzas to the high school Christmas craft fair."

He nodded. "Which we are."

She said, "It's the music school."

Ezra shook his head. She said, "Ezra, I saw the calendar. The music school's got Christmas performances all day."

He said, "I saw the calendar too. You're mixing up which school is which."

Lacey walked into the business office. "Castleton Music School. Seventy-five pizzas."

Ezra wiped off his hands and brought up the calendar on the computer. "Hartwell High School. Sixty pizzas. Barrett wrote it down wrong."

Lacey said, "I confirmed it with them myself last week. Music school and high school are two separate things."

"Which you shouldn't have, because the Hartwell High School Christmas craft fair is an annual thing. It's been in in the calendar since last December."

Lacey snapped, "Are you saying no one but you knows how to read a calendar?"and then went to the electronic calendar to look at the day. It said, of course, Hartwell High School Craft Fair.

Well. Wasn't this about to get fun?

Ezra huffed. "And you didn't bother checking the calendar before confirming it with them?"

She gestured. "You might notice the calendar in your hands has nothing else on it other than the music school."

"Well, as of now, we're in panic mode." He glared at her. "I'm calling Greg. I'll tell him you got your wish, because today, we're making a hundred seventy-five pizzas."

Lacey pulled the finished dough out of the Hobart and started reloading the machine. This was Uncle Barrett's fault. He was the one with multiple calendars and multiple streams of information. The first thing she'd need to do was streamline all their scheduling into one process so this didn't happen again.

Still—today. The craft fair needed most of their deliveries between noon and two. The country club was going to go later than that. The music school was an all-day affair.

Ezra put down the phone without speaking, and she said, "That doesn't sound good."

"Yeah, he didn't answer, and he's not reading his texts. He may be in Boston for all I know." Ezra stripped off his sweatshirt, leaving him in short sleeves. "It's all you and me."

A hundred seventy-five pizzas, and they were at a low point in supplies. Lacey braced herself. "Let's do this thing."

Ezra got the oven to temp while the doughs were proofing. Lacey prepped the toppings. Still no Greg. Shelly confirmed she'd be in early. That left the entire kitchen to Lacey and Ezra to double a normal day's output.

Lacey didn't update the social media as they worked. What would she say? "Due to a mixup, the Loveless One Hundred is almost two hundred, but we're sure it will be fine." Nope. Best leave that out.

On the other hand, between pies, Ezra did post an update. "Loveless to the rescue! After an ill-timed kitchen fire, you can sample our Wreath Pizza and donate to children's cancer research at the country club."

He knew how to handle these things. He barely broke stride while doing it.

Shelly was in and out the whole day. Lacey parceled out the toppings, but they were going to come up short on the mushrooms. They might end up needing to locally source them by sending Shelly up to the grocery store to clear an entire shelf.

Ezra worked like a machine. For all that he'd protested about not doing more than a hundred pizzas a day, he was nailing it now. They had dough proofing on every surface, and he was prepping pizzas and cycling them in and out of the oven like a pizza king. At every moment, he knew where everything sat and in what state it was.

More than that, he knew without checking exactly what Lacey was doing, whether it was topping the pizzas or spreading cheese or tracking which pizzas had gotten delivered to which sites. When toppings got short, he didn't question when she reconfigured how much to put on which pies.

He trusted her. Now, when it counted, he trusted enough to let her fit in around his work. At the same time, he was modifying his operations to include her.

This was teamwork at its best. This was a partnership.

Ezra turned on the radio, and as he worked, he sang. He'd never sang for her before. Lacey didn't want to join him and ruin it, but eventually did—and he didn't go silent.

Shelly never stopped for longer than it took to reload her delivery bag. They all took a quick break at the halfway point, eating (ironically) fast food that Shelly had grabbed after her last dropoff. "Oh, and look," Shelly said, "the craft fair organizer tried to hold a sprig of mistletoe over my head and give me a kiss."

Ezra glared over from the counter. "He did what?"

With a flourish, she produced a pretty bundle of green leaves and red ribbon. "Oh, don't worry. I told him I was keeping this in order to preserve the consent of every other woman at the craft fair, and if he didn't watch it, he'd get his picture up on the Loveless social media with a discussion of how not to treat your delivery driver." She rolled her eyes as she tossed the mistletoe sprig onto the opposite counter. "Three women applauded, and he slunk away."

Lacey looked around. "Do we need to strike the craft fair from our list of customers?"

Ezra shrugged. "There's a different director every year, so I'll just make sure the craft fair committee knows to strike this one person as someone we'd work with in the future."

Lacey gave him a thumbs-up. "Thank you."

Ezra muttered, "It's classier than handling it the old fashioned way."

Then it was back to making pizzas.

Lacey called out the remaining numbers every time Shelly did a delivery. It was scant relief to be in the double digits, far better when they got below fifty, then two dozen, and finally the last batch. Shelly bagged it up, and she was out the door.

Ezra stood with his palms against the counter, head down, breathing hard. They were both drenched in sweat. Lacey locked the door for the oven, then turned to Ezra again. His arms curved with muscles, and his apron hung loose around his waist and neck. Although exhausted, he looked ready for anything.

Well, anything except what she was about to do. She slipped away to grab a folder from the office.

When she got back, Ezra finally looked around the kitchen. "I know we need to get things cleaned up, but I need a break."

"Hey, time to lean, and then time to clean." Lacey sat on the floor, knees tucked up, the folder dangling between two fingers. She'd probably gotten flour all over the seat of her jeans because flour got everywhere in a pizza kitchen. Even standard nonslip shoes didn't work here.

Ezra laughed, then sat across from her. "Today was forty-five hours long."

"Without a break," Lacey said, sitting taller. "But you did great."

Ezra said, "*We* did great. I'm not the only one working here."

He looked aside, though, as if to hide the sadness that flashed across his face.

Lacey said, "So, on the heels of this victory, do you remember I said I wanted to run something by you?"

Ezra's mouth twitched. "Yes, but maybe we should let this stand as the high point for a little longer before we blow everything up, don't you think?"

Lacey frowned. "You have that little faith in me?"

"It's that I know something you don't know." Ezra drew a deep breath. "So... We agree the problem is that Loveless can't afford two full-time salaries on top of everything else. And you're going to need a salary as the new owner, so that leaves me."

Lacey's heart stuttered. "Wait— Ezra, stop."

He shook his head. "Hear me out. I have a job offer from Jake's. Same number of hours, comparable salary, all that. I'll be fine, and you know everything you need to know to keep the place running, so you'll be fine, too. It's not like I'm the pizzeria's beating heart—"

"—Except that you *are* the pizzeria's beating heart!" Lacey's voice pitched up. "You can't quit. There's something I need to tell you."

His mouth tightened, but he stopped.

"I talked to Uncle Barrett." She tried to catch her breath.

104

"Because none of this is right." Ezra didn't interrupt. "He shouldn't be giving the place to me." Lacey's eyes stung. "I know he's got no business sense, but the fact is, all along, the heart and soul of Loveless Pizza has been Ezra Blake. It's been nothing else."

Ezra started.

Lacey held up a hand. "Even though he had the idea, you made the idea workable. You took every one of his stupid decisions, and you capitalized on them."

Ezra frowned, but he seemed puzzled.

Lacey said, "You're not just an employee. You're the co-founder."

He opened his hand. "And...?"

"And it's not fair to shut you out. You've been right all along. This business was your project from the start. He'd never have gotten the doors open if it hadn't been for you, and he wouldn't have kept the doors open a week."

Ezra smirked. "At least a month. Give him a little credit."

"None whatsoever. He admits he had no idea what he was doing." Lacey tucked her knees tighter. "When I told him all this, he agreed. He can't just give me his pizzeria because it's not really his pizzeria to begin with."

Ezra tilted his head and raised a hand. "Except on paper."

She lifted the folder. "On *this* paper, I happen to have words that would make you and me together the co-owners of Loveless Pizza."

"What?" Ezra scrambled up. "But— How can you?"

"Because it's not as if I deserve to own a pizzeria. I'm not giving up anything that was mine in the first place. If anyone deserves it, it's you." Lacey blinked hard. "So—you can't just go work for Jake's Pizza." Her voice broke. "You can't go work for him when you own the competition."

Ezra raised his hands. "I didn't know you were thinking about any of this when I called him."

Lacey said, "You asked to go work for the enemy?"

"If it saved Loveless, yes, I would march myself right over to the enemy and wage war against Hartwell House of Pizza, which really is more Jake's direct competition."

Lacey huffed. "Do you have to criticize everything I say?"

"I think that's in the paperwork," Ezra said, so she handed him the folder. "If it's not, I'll have to include it. *Every twenty-five minutes, Ezra must issue one criticism of...*" He stopped.

Lacey said, tired, "Go ahead."

He said, "Do I get to criticize your name? Because either your uncle got it wrong, or I do. You're a Lovelace?"

Lacey said, "Don't even try to pronounce my first name."

Ezra pulled out his phone. "No, I need to pronounce this. A-o-i-f-e. Pronounced, *EE-fa*. Irish. Means, *Lovely lady*." He looked her up and down. "Okay, I'll grant that."

She sighed. "You're so generous, allowing me to use my own given name."

"Now I know why you're so offended by Loveless." He was having way too good a time right now. "Because it's your actual name, and unlike your uncle, you care."

She said, "And everyone can pronounce Barrett. By age seven, I'd given up."

"Aren't you full of mystery?" Ezra sighed. "Okay, but even so. How do we get around the 'can't afford two full time salaries' problem? Fun as it would be, I assume *EE-fa Lovelace* is not planning on living in my car." He hesitated, then raised his eyebrows. "Although if you want to spend time with me in my car, I can think of a few—"

"Quit that!" Lacey snatched the folder back from him and waved it at him as though she were swatting away an insect. "We'll have about a year to figure out new revenue streams. You'll have veto power, but you'll see all the information. I'm not the only one who can make changes. We just proved we can make more pizzas per day than we have been, although I'd rather stop short of a hundred seventy-five."

Ezra blurted out, "A food truck."

Of all ten trillion possible word combinations in the English language, those were not in the top ten percent of words Lacey had expected to hear from Ezra. "Repeat that?"

He got to his knees and moved closer, gesturing with his hands. "A food truck. I've always wanted to take Loveless to events like the ones we were hosting today, only we'd park outside and make the pizzas onsite."

Lacey breathed, "Oh... And that opens us up to all sorts of events, not just craft fairs."

Ezra came closer. "Outdoor concerts, blood drives, backyard weddings, town spirit festivals—"

"Do they even sell brick oven pizza trucks?" Lacey squinted at him. "Because the last thing I want is to make the news with a flaming food truck rolling down Route 186."

Ezra snorted. "Yes, they do brick oven pizza trucks. We'd need a business loan, but that would be your area of expertise."

Lacey tilted her head and raised a hand, palm outward. "A moment, my good sir. What if the brick oven pizza truck had the occasional farm-to-table event?"

Ezra pressed his palm against hers and entwined their

fingers. "You mean, someone books it for precisely that reason?"

He moved closer to her, and she relaxed back into the cabinet, letting her knees drop. "A very specific farm-to-table event, that way everyone knows what they're getting into."

Ezra had drawn very close now. When he spoke, his voice was low and his presence intoxicating. "Do you think people always know what they're getting into?"

Lacey brushed a hand along his cheek. "I don't usually."

He guided her hand close to his lips. "And now?"

She grinned at him. "Especially not now."

He kissed her hand, but this time, it was for real. He started with his lips on the back of her hand, then worked toward her wrist. He didn't get up to her arm before she tugged him toward her, and then she kissed his mouth.

His presence overpowered her restraint, but she pulled back enough to say, "But I'm willing to give it a go."

Then she let him keep kissing her. Shelly would be back soon. They'd have to clean an entire trashed kitchen. They'd need to figure out the paperwork and change all the names on the accounts. They'd need to figure out funding. They needed so many things, but for the moment, she just needed Ezra close, so that's what they had.

Epilogue

"We're going to sell out," Lacey said as she pulled a pizza from the oven, then started slicing.

Ezra called from the assembly station, "Santa's going to be here in ten minutes. Should be fine."

Lacey plated up pizza slices for the family at the window of the food truck, the kids laughing at the mozzarella snowmen centered on each slice. She glanced up the line and decided they'd probably have enough pizzas to get through this—but Santa had better come to town soon, otherwise there would be a bunch of disappointed would-be pizza eaters.

She and Ezra had worked for the entire Hartwell Christmas Eve festival at the town park while families looked at the displays, and music played at the gazebo. Kids were excited and their parents looked tense, but most people seemed to be having a good time. Further out, couples walked around the pond on a path strung with lights. It would be nice to walk that path with Ezra, but instead they were here, at what she'd affectionately dubbed "food vendor alley."

What a difference a year had made.

Ezra had been right about the food truck. It had taken a bit of coaxing to get the loan they needed, and then a little longer to get the truck, but here it was, with a wood-fired oven the same as at the Loveless kitchen, and their logo across the front. They sold pizza by the slice, and as an interesting side effect, she actually got to talk to their regulars.

"I love your social media," the next woman gushed. "You make it fun to order dinner."

Lacey said, "It's all Ezra."

Ezra passed behind her, saying, "It's half Ezra, and half Lacey."

Once word got out about the food truck, they'd gotten booked nearly every weekend of the summer. One town had requested they show up for every performance of their summer concert series, and another town had them serving lunch for the first day of school.

Also—yes—sometimes they got booked for their farm-to-table pizzas. And (ahem) when they offered farm-to-table premium pizzas? They sold out.

Lacey chuckled to herself as she ran a credit card. *Take that, Ezra!*

Tonight, customers came to the window with gloves on their hands and their breath visible. The pizza steamed as it left the oven-warmed truck, and Lacey alternated between too hot and too cold as she moved between the pizza oven and the sales window.

Ezra moved about the truck, too. They'd learned to work together so well, each anticipating the other's moves, each working around the other while creating, cooking, and serving the pizzas. They made a great partnership.

Ezra squeezed her hand as he moved back past her again. They made a great partnership, but they also made a great couple.

Jingle bells began sounding, and Lacey sighed because that meant Santa—and Santa's arrival meant half the line dispersed so the kids could watch Santa's grand entrance into the park. They'd make it to the end of the evening.

When they cleared the line, Ezra stood behind her and wrapped his arms around her waist. "I told you we'd have enough."

"We cut it pretty close." She turned toward him, and he kissed her. "How do you think Greg and Shelly are doing back at the shop?"

"They're fine. Greg's always fine." Ezra chuckled. "It's Shelly I'm worried about."

Lacey hesitated. "Driving all over the place?"

"Her and Greg. I think something's up."

Lacey straightened, and he held her closer. Now that they weren't moving, it was getting chillier inside the truck.

"Is she crushing on him?"

"She won't admit it." Ezra bent toward Lacey, and his breath against her neck didn't do anything to diminish the chills running over her. "And Greg's oblivious in general, so this might get interesting."

Across the park, Santa was yelling "Ho, ho, ho!" into a loudspeaker, and the kids were chanting it back.

Lacey said, "Do we need to do another special pizza? An engagement pizza?"

Ezra murmured into her ear, "Do we dot it with little onion rings?"

He ran his hands up her arms to her shoulders and then back down. Lacey felt abruptly warmer.

Ezra nuzzled her neck. "What would you want on your engagement pizza?"

She said, "I'm traditional. The man should make the engagement pizza for me, and then he should get on one knee to serve it."

Ezra laughed, and then Lacey turned to him, putting her arms over his shoulders. "It's been quite a year, hasn't it?"

"So many things changed," Ezra said.

She chuckled. "And you didn't want anything to change."

He frowned. "They haven't all been bad changes."

She arched her eyebrows. "Any good ones?"

He thought. "Well, snowman pizzas seem to be a good change," and she chucked him in the shoulder. "I don't know, I just can't come up with—"

She stepped back and folded her arms. "You'd better be careful with whatever you say next."

Ezra reached for her hands, and she let him. He said, "You stepped into my pizzeria, and you changed my life. You recognized things about me that even I didn't know, and you were brave enough to take a chance on me. You wanted to work together with me even though we started out at odds with one another. This past year has been the most amazing year of my life, and it's all because of you."

He squeezed her hands. "Will you marry me?"

Lacey started. "Marry you?"

He tugged her toward him. "Marry me. We're already business partners. Let's be partners through and through. We've had one amazing year. Let's have an amazing lifetime."

Lacey stepped into his embrace. At her back was the warmth of the wood-fired stove, and all around her was the work they'd created together.

"Yes," she said. "I'll marry you."

He kissed her, and she closed her eyes to savor the moment.

When he released her, she said, "Wait, don't I get an engagement pizza?" and Ezra burst into laughter. "I'm sure I was supposed to get an engagement pizza!"

Just then, the lights flared on at the town Christmas tree, and the kids cheered. A pair of customers approached the truck, and Ezra stepped toward the window.

She slipped up behind him just before the customers arrived, and gave him a hug. "I destroyed Loveless Pizza after all—because we're no longer loveless."

Ezra took the customers' order while Lacey slipped another pizza into the wood-fired oven.

THANK YOU!

Thank you so much for reading about Ezra and Lacey! I had so much fun with this story, and I hope you did, too. I hope you're planning to order a pizza tonight. A beautiful wood-fired pizza with a crisp crust dotted with leopard spots, melty cheese, and all the perfect toppings.

I want to thank my writing partners at the Metrowest Writers Guild for their encouragement and suggestions. Also thank you to the other Mistletoe Kisses authors, who've all been an amazing group.

Did you love the book? If so, please consider leaving a review at Amazon, Goodreads, Bookbub, or anywhere else you like to leave reviews. Also, it's helpful when readers share the books they're reading on social media. (Not just mine—everyone's! I love to see what other people are enjoying, and most of my reading comes from other people's recommendations.)

If you'd like to keep in touch with me, **please join my "Maddie Mondays."** About twice a month (on Mondays, you'll notice,) I'll share a funny anecdote from my chaotic life, a recommendation for something I'm reading, knitting, or otherwise thinking you'll enjoy, and information about my other stories. You can find that at https://stats.sender.net/forms/erBXBe/view

A PAPER SNOWFLAKE CHRISTMAS

*Do you want more Christmas love? Tuck up under the blankets for **A Paper Snowflake Christmas.***

Marlie can't afford to join her family on their Christmas trip, so her friends will host their own Christmas. The question is, where?

Enter Devin, former mischief-maker and Marlie's childhood crush, who volunteers his home for their holidays. He's still got a wicked grin and a luscious voice. The catch? He's got custody of his four-year-old nephew, a boy who's never had a real Christmas.

Years ago, Marlie kept her head down, folding origami cranes and cutting paper snowflakes. This year, everyone's caught up in the rush giving a preschooler his first magical Christmas...but if she gets brave enough to unfold her paper snowflake heart, maybe Marlie can have one, too.